**OPERATOR 5:
REVOLT OF THE DEVIL MEN**

SECRET SERVICE OPERATOR #5

AMERICA'S UNDERCOVER ACE

REVOLT OF THE DEVIL MEN

By Curtis Steele

POPULAR PUBLICATIONS • 2023

© 1938, 2023 Argosy Communications, Inc. All rights reserved.
Authorized and produced under license.

PUBLISHING HISTORY

"Revolt of the Devil Men" originally appeared in the May/June, 1938 (Vol. 10, No. 3) issue of *Operator #5* magazine. Copyright © 2023 by Argosy Communications, Inc. All rights reserved.

ALL RIGHTS RESERVED

No part of this book may be reproduced or utilized in any form or by any means, electronic or mechanical, without permission in writing from the publisher.

This edition has been marked via subtle changes, so anyone who reprints from this collection is committing a violation of copyright.

Visit POPULARPUBLICATIONS.COM for more books like this.

CHAPTER 1
RED REVOLT

THE MOB was ominously silent. There were more than a thousand men in that swiftly gathered throng. Armed with rifles, clubs and revolvers, they were moving down along the waterfront, muttering—not shouting. It was easy to see that their objective was the great rectangle of warehouses at the Battery, which had been erected by President Sheridan to store up food and ammunition for the city of New York.

Now, as the forefront of the mob approached the wire fence surrounding the rectangle, their murmuring voices blended into a cumulative whisper of bitterness. They came to a swaying halt, and pressed upon each other, watching the thin line of military police who had drawn up to face them.

Young Captain Andy Bretton, in command of the detail, stood out in front of his men, tensely watching the mob. Perhaps a hundred yards separated the leaders of the throng from Captain Bretton. "Stand back!" he shouted.

Someone in the mob laughed raucously. "Where do you get that stuff, Bretton? We want food. Our rations are too small. Take your soldiers away before we walk over them. We're gonna take what we want out of those warehouses!"

Andy Bretton frowned. He saw the man who had spoken—a heavy-set, bullet-headed fellow, who wore a brown shirt. Upon the sleeve of that shirt was embroidered the figure of a hawk.

Bretton knew the man—Fritz Koller, a leader of the Brown Guard Party, which had recently been inciting the populace to discontent.

For a moment, Bretton entertained the idea of striding

REVOLT OF THE DEVIL MEN

forward into that mob, and arresting Koller. But the Brown Shirt leader was far back, and on the side lines. He would not be thrusting himself into the front of the fighting. There were

The machine-gun bullets drummed upward!

other Brown Shirts in the mob, too. Bretton could spot them, scattered here and there, urging the others on to attack.

The captain moved slowly along his line of men until he was at the extreme right. His men were standing taut, rifles ready. If the mob moved closer, Bretton would have to order them to fire. They would kill many—and those men in the throng were Americans. Bretton swallowed hard. He looked around desperately, hoping that someone would intervene.

He heard Koller shouting, "Come on, boys! They won't shoot. Let's go!" Koller wasn't going to lead the charge—he was well in back now.

The crowd began to move forward, slowly. Those in the front rank realized that they would receive the brunt of the soldiers' first volley. But the throng behind was pressing them forward. In a moment they would yield to that pressure, and charge.

Andy Bretton called out desperately, "Wait! You fools, don't you realize what you're doing? The food in these warehouses is insurance against famine. If you should succeed in taking it now, you'd be signing your own death warrant. Won't—"

But his voice was lost in the sudden rumbling sound that came from the mob. They were pushing forward. Captain Bretton's face was drawn with pain. He couldn't bring himself to order his troops to fire against these Americans. They were not wicked, in the main, merely misguided and egged on to this mad attack by the insidious work of the Brown Shirts.

Instead of ordering a volley, he shouted to his troops, "Retire behind the gate!"

His men were obviously relieved, too. Before the mob got

up enough momentum to sweep toward them, the troops had filed swiftly in through the gate. Bretton was the last one in, and, just as he swung the gate shut, a rifle barked behind him. The bullet flattened itself against an iron stanchion, and Bretton slammed the gate.

The troops spread out in the courtyard. The mob, now infuriated, rushed forward, reached the wire fence, and pressed against it. The Brown Shirts were eagerly exhorting them to scale the fence. Koller had a megaphone and was shouting through it, "See—they won't shoot! Come on—over the fence!"

THE COURTYARD into which Bretton's men had retreated was in the shape of a great rectangle, flanked on three sides by the low long sheds of the warehouses. The fourth side was open, facing north into the town, and it was at this side that the mob was pressing.

There were three warehouses, built to hug the shore so that their rear exits faced onto the docks of the North River, and the Upper Bay. The warehouses themselves were only two stories high. On the roof of each of the three buildings there were three-foot buttresses from behind which eight machine guns commanded the courtyard.

Bretton glanced up toward them, saw that they were fully manned, ready to lay down a barrage that would effectually stop the mob once they had passed the fence.

But it would be slaughter—and these were Americans. Many were relatives of the very soldiers here in the courtyard, the machine gunners above. Captain Bretton's whole attitude mirrored the indecision he felt. His mood was not slow

OPERATOR 5

in conveying itself to the mob. They sensed that Bretton was unwilling to fire upon them. Fritz Koller and the other Brown Shirts had counted on this when they egged the mob onward. Now they were clamoring for the others to climb the fence.

Two, three, a half dozen were already clambering up, to straddle the top. In an instant they would overwhelm the small guard, without the firing of a shot. Food which had been stored for almost a year would be carried away in an hour.

Also, a disaster such as this might spell ruin not only for the city of New York, but also for the rest of the nation. America was just recovering from the most devastating war that had ever been waged within her borders. Only a year ago we had driven out the last of the armies of the Purple Empire, had sent them scampering back across the Atlantic.*

---

* AUTHOR'S NOTE: For an account of the history of the Purple War, the reader is referred to previous issues of this periodical. Those of our readers who are familiar with the history of the period referred to already know that America came very close to becoming a vassal state of the Purple Empire. The inception of the Purple Empire lay originally in a military state of central Europe whose dictator had employed the military machine of his country to further the conquest of the rest of Europe, and of Asia. Then, after becoming Emperor of all of those conquered nations and uniting them under the title of the Purple Empire, the Purple Emperor had sent his mighty hosts against America. This country, having followed always the policy of peaceful ways, had no military machine of comparable strength to that of the invader. Our Defense Forces were soon driven back across the country to the Pacific Coast, and the Black Days set in for America—days when American citi-

REVOLT OF THE DEVIL MEN

For two years the Purple Emperor's hordes had ravaged with sword and fire from coast to coast. Only through the efforts of President Sheridan, aided by a small band of loyal Americans, headed by the man known as Operator 5, had we at last succeeded in recovering our liberty. But we had been without resources, our mines and oil wells destroyed, our sources of power and light crippled. America was going through a period of primitive pioneering work that required as much self-sacrifice and self-abnegation as had been demanded of the original pioneers who had settled the land.

All these things did not pass through Captain Andy Bretton's mind in logical sequence; but he felt them poignantly in the moment when he saw the leaders of that mob scaling the fence.

zens were forced into concentration camps and labor battalions, and when the victorious troops of the Purple Emperor visited rape and murder upon the luckless residents of the Occupied Territory.

Then there had sprung up the spark of resistance, fostered throughout all those trying times by the man known as Operator 5. It was Operator 5—known to his intimate friends as Jimmy Christopher—who brought about the first defeat of the Purple Armies at the Battle of the Continental Divide; and who subsequently, by the use of resource and strategy and courage, encompassed the death of Emperor Rudolph, and the ignominious retreat of the Purple Army from our shores. This story is the story of America's tribulations; but it is also the story of Operator 5, and of Diane Elliot, and of the boy Tim Donovan, and of those other members of that small band without whose daring and courage America might not be upon the map of the world today!

OPERATOR 5

The decision was his, and his alone, to make—whether to order his troops to fire upon these Americans and slaughter them, or to allow the mob to seize the stores of food and ammunition which were the life-blood of a struggling nation.

Vividly, all those past events flashed through Bretton's brain, just as a man's whole life is said to rush through his subconscious vision in the instant before death. He was only a young man, promoted recently to a captaincy because of valor on the field of battle. He was impressionable, a true lover of America. His arm was half-raised to give the order to fire. A good number of the mob were over the fence, opening the gate for the rest. A single volley would never disperse them. It would require volley upon volley—probably mean that he would have to order the machine guns into action, to mow them down.

Bretton did not have the cold brutality that dictator's possess—the heartless, adamant will to succeed that enabled a man like Bonaparte to turn his artillery upon the Paris mob and thus launch himself upon the career of conquest that made Europe a shambles. Bretton had too much sensitiveness for that. He could envisage the torn bodies of those men littering the pavement of the courtyard after his machine guns swept it. He knew in that instant that he could never give the order to fire.

Now the mob was streaming in through the gate, and Captain Bretton's riflemen were looking to him for orders. It was one of those moments which are sprinkled throughout history, when the fate of a nation has hung in the balance—and when the decisive action of a single man has changed the course of recorded history. Certainly such a moment was here now. The food and ammunition in those warehouses would provide the life-blood for a struggling country, fighting to regain its destroyed civilization. Without that food the coming year would be a nightmare of privation. Men would have to grub in the ground for food instead of building factories and mining coal and building sanitary equipment.

And it was in that instant that help came to Captain Bretton from a source he had forgotten.

Suddenly, one of the riflemen called to him urgently. "Captain Bretton—look, down there!"

Bretton turned, and gazed in the direction in which the rifleman was pointing, along the alley between Warehouses Number One and Two. The alley ran down to the river, where a motor launch was tying up at the dock.

A single figure was leaping out of that launch, running toward the courtyard. Andy Bretton allowed his breath to escape in a long gasp of relief. The shouts of the mob were still in his ears, but he did not hear them. His eyes gleamed eagerly.

"Operator 5!" he exclaimed.

THE MAN who now appeared out of the alley had the build of an athlete, with wide shoulders that tapered down to narrow hips. He wore the simple tunic of a captain of Intelligence, but there was that in the firm set of his lips, the angle of his jaw, the flash of his eyes, that belied the lowly rank indicated by his uniform.

OPERATOR 5

At sight of him, the riflemen lost their tenseness, and the machine gunners on the roofs of the warehouses relaxed.

But it was his effect upon the mob that was most startling. In the moment before his appearance, their voices had been raised in infuriated shouts, in catcalls at the riflemen, mingled with the exhortations of Fritz Koller and the other Brown Shirts.

Abruptly, all that ended. The shouting and catcalls died down. Koller's voice dwindled, was silent. A great hush descended upon the courtyard.

Operator 5 looked neither to the right nor the left. He strode forward toward the front ranks of the mob, eyes burning into the leaders. He stopped when he was within twenty feet of them, and let his gaze sweep along the ragged line. His lips twisted in scorn.

"You fools!" he said, in a voice so low that it could barely be heard. "Don't you realize what you're doing? The food in these warehouses was captured from the Purple Empire. It is concentrated food, calculated to support a huge army for a year. For us, it would be enough to feed the nation for many months. And you want to take it and destroy it—consume it overnight!"

The men in the forefront of the mob shuffled under his gaze. No one answered for a moment. Then Fritz Koller, seeing the hold that Operator 5 was gaining upon them, raised his voice.

"This is a free country!" he shouted. "President Sheridan has been starving us, handing out short rations. And now he wants to send half of this food out to the rest of the country. We want it kept here. We refuse to starve for the sake of people a thousand miles away!"

REVOLT OF THE DEVIL MEN

Andy Bretton was watching the scene, tautly. He had little hope that Operator 5 would be able to stem the mob. He knew that those Brown Shirt *provocateurs* would continue to fan the flame of the mob's passions until they stormed the warehouses. He was sure that Operator 5 must also realize this, and wondered what he hoped to accomplish by talking to them in this way. It might delay matters for a few minutes, but inevitably the attack would come. Those men were worked up to a fever pitch. They knew that the small force of riflemen and machine gunners would not fire upon them—and the Brown Shirts were egging them on. To Andy Bretton, it seemed that Operator 5's attempt to stop them was mere folly, and would only result in his being killed in the first wave of the charging mob.

But just then Captain Bretton happened to glance behind him toward the alley, and the thing he saw there caused the blood to race through his veins, feverishly.

A young woman and a boy were trundling a small handtruck toward the courtyard. The handtruck was loaded with four large wooden cases.

Captain Bretton knew both the boy and the young woman. They were Tim Donovan, and Diane Elliot. The boy, barely out of his teens, had been the constant companion of Operator 5 for the past two or three years. There were many grown men who would have given their right arms for the privilege of having the record of daring accomplishments possessed by freckled-faced Tim Donovan. The young woman, Diane Elliot, was the fiancée of Operator 5. She was also a member of the small band who had fought at the side of Operator 5 through the two long years of

OPERATOR 5

the Purple War, and whose courage and self-sacrifice had made possible the final defeat of the Purple Emperor.

Their present purpose was not so clear to Andy Bretton. He could see that the cases loaded on the hand truck contained dynamite from Warehouse Number Three. Diane and Tim had landed from the motor launch with Operator 5, of course, and must have hurried to the rear of the warehouse to load the handtruck. What they intended to accomplish with that dynamite was more than Bretton could figure. He saw them stop the truck just short of the courtyard. Tim Donovan ripped a board off one of the cases, inserted a short fuse, and lit it. His blood ran cold. Those four cases of explosive were enough to tear apart every brick in the warehouse buildings and destroy every living being in the courtyard.

OPERATOR 5 was still facing the mob. He was using every bit of his eloquence to turn them from their purpose. "Many of you men fought with me at the Battle of Hoboken," he was saying earnestly. "You risked your lives then and you were glad to do it for America. Now, the President asks much less of you. He asks only that you limit your rations, so that the rest of the country may be fed. In the West, and in the Southwest, there is a drought. Those people out there fought just as bravely as we did, and they're entitled to be fed. Let's all pull together, and the country will come out of this—"

He was interrupted by Fritz Koller who shouted, "To hell with all that. If we don't get fed properly, we don't work. Ain't that right, boys?"

The mob answered with a wild shout, and surged forward, as

REVOLT OF THE DEVIL MEN

if to engulf Operator 5. Andy Bretton and the riflemen started to run to his aid, but they stopped short, for Operator 5 had raised his arm in the air. Without looking behind him, he shouted, *"Okay, Tim!"*

The leaders of the mob broke their stride, wondering what he meant. In that moment of hesitation, Tim Donovan and Diane Elliot came out of the alley, trundling their handcart. The sputtering fuse in the wooden case was clearly visible to everyone in the mob. A strange sigh—half of fear, half of wonder—went up from them.

Still without turning around, Operator addressed them again. "There's dynamite in those cases, men. In two minutes the fuse will burn down, and you'll all be blown out of here."

So great was his confidence in Tim Donovan and Diane Elliot that he did not even turn to see if they were there. When they had approached the dock in the motor launch, he had sized up the situation and given them swift instructions. From the habit of years—from the habit which that small band had developed of meeting emergencies swiftly and efficiently—he knew that they were there, without looking.

Now he faced down that mob. "Every one of us will be dead in two minutes," he said solemnly. "Rather than see you ruin the country by taking our only supply of reserve food, *I'd rather destroy you* and—I'm ready to die with you!"

He paused, and smiled. "Now, if any of you want to come ahead anyway, why you're welcome!"

He stepped back and waved to them.

The mob stood there transfixed, eyes glued to that sputter-

OPERATOR 5

ing fuse. Not a man of them doubted that there was dynamite in those boxes. To make doubly sure that they would believe it, Tim Donovan, with a strained smile on his youthful face, ripped off the top boards of the other cases, and lifted out one of the sticks, held it up for them to see.

That settled it. The mob broke and ran pell-mell for the gate. They pushed, jostled, crowded, in their frantic efforts to get through. Many of them scaled the fence, going out as they had come in. In the van of those who ran were the Brown Shirts. Fritz Koller, forehead covered with sweat, was among the first to climb the fence. In less than the two minutes which Operator 5 had given them, the last of the mob was outside the courtyard.

Operator 5 smiled. He nodded to Tim Donovan, who stooped quickly forward, and pinched out the fuse, which was now down to a quarter inch. Tim Donovan mopped his forehead, and grinned.

"Gosh, Jimmy," he said to Operator 5, "that was close!"

Operator 5 didn't answer him. He had kept his eyes on the back of the brown-shirted Fritz Koller. He did not know the man by name, but had spotted him as the chief instigator of the mob. He wanted that man for questioning.

He waved to Captain Bretton. "Take over, Andy. Close the gates. Shoot if you're attacked again!"

He headed out through the gate, into the milling crowd in the street. They made way before him, none attempting to interfere with him. Another man might have hesitated to trust himself among these men whom he had just driven off, but Operator 5 pushed through them boldly, never looking to either side.

He kept his gaze fixed on the retreating backs of several of the Brown Shirts, who were already turning into one of the side streets.

CHAPTER 2
TRAITORS TO TRAP

HE QUICKLY caught up with them, and came abreast of their leader. He was running easily, his well-muscled, lithe physique hardly overtaxing itself to catch the bullet-headed man. Jimmy pressed close to this one, and the man did not even bother to turn his head, thinking it was one of his own men.

Jimmy crowded him to the wall, and the others, now behind them, shouted a warning. The leader looked around for the first time, and a startled expression came into his square face. He reached for his gun, but Operator 5's hand flashed swiftly up and down, and rammed into his side; holding a snub-nosed automatic.

The man gasped, and let his hand fall away from the holster.

Jimmy smiled thinly, saying, "That's right, Mr. Brown Shirt. Stand still!"

He forced the other to halt against the wall, and swung around in time to face the other Brown Shirts who now were puffing toward them. Their eyes were ugly, and it seemed for an instant that their momentum would carry them squarely into Operator 5. But Jimmy's gun poked out at them, and they abruptly broke off their swift strides, coming to a halt within a few feet.

OPERATOR 5

Jimmy Christopher reached up with his left hand and gripped the leader's collar in hard fingers, while he menaced the others with his automatic.

"I am arresting this man in the name of the Provisional Government of the United States," he said. "Anyone who interferes will be subject to military law!"

The men held back, not so much because of Jimmy Christopher's announcement as because of the threat of his gun. But the prisoner squirmed in his grasp and shouted, "Take him, men. He's only one—"

Operator 5 twisted his fingers in the man's collar so that the fellow choked for breath, the words breaking off into a gasp.

The others spread out, holding their guns ready, and coming at Jimmy from two angles. Jimmy Christopher thrust his prisoner forward and swung his gun around in a semicircle. From the direction of the waterfront the shouts and cries of the dispersing mob were still coming. But here the Brown Shirts were closing in, silent and deadly.

There were five of them, and Jimmy Christopher could not hope to take his prisoner past them with his one gun. He took a swift step backward, placing his prisoner in front of him as a shield. At the same time he thrust the barrel of his gun against the Brown Shirt's ribs.

"Call your dogs off," he snapped, "or I'll empty this gun into you!"

The Brown Shirt leader stiffened perceptibly. He was still gasping for air, and Jimmy loosened his hold slightly. "Now, talk to them!" His voice was cold and hard as the muzzle of the gun, and the prisoner must have sensed the steely determination of his captor.

He called out hoarsely to the advancing Brown Shirts, "Stop, men! He'll kill me. Better—leave him alone!"

Jimmy's narrowed eyes watched the slow, reluctant retreat of the Brown Shirts. They backed slowly across the street, keeping their eyes fixed on the two men. They were spread out now, and it was difficult for Jimmy Christopher to keep track of them all. He was sure there had been five of them at the start, but now there were only four. One of them must have slipped into a doorway, to snipe at him when he started away.

Operator 5 smiled tightly. This man must be an important leader of the Brown Shirts, if they were so anxious to keep him from arrest. He retained his grip on the man's collar, and moved quickly to the right, about five paces. There was a doorway here, and before the slow-thinking Brown Shirts had guessed his intention, he reached behind him, tried the door, and pushed it open. Then he yanked his prisoner backward, slipped into the hallway, and slammed the door.

The men outside uttered maddened shouts, and rushed forward. Jimmy Christopher grimly poked his prisoner in the back, and said, "Get going!"

THEY RACED down the hallway, with the cries of the frustrated Brown Shirts ringing in their ears. Jimmy's gun was never out of the other's back, and when the man hesitated once, breaking his stride, Operator 5 thrust the muzzle hard against his spine. In a moment, they were at the rear of the building, and out into the back yard.

OPERATOR 5

Jimmy forced his prisoner ahead of him, through an alley, and then into the street behind. For a moment they were free of the pursuit of the other Brown Shirts. His prisoner turned a sweating countenance to him.

"Look here. Why don't you be reasonable? You can't hold me for anything. What's the charge against me?"

"Inciting to riot," Jimmy told him grimly. He pushed the man roughly ahead. "Get going before your friends come through that alley. It'll be too bad for you if they stop us." His eyes were cold.

The other held back. "Dammit, you can't arrest me like this. My name is Koller—Fritz Koller. I'm a well known man. Where's your authority—"

Operator 5 goaded him with the automatic. "This is enough authority for the time being. I'll show you more later."

They rounded the corner just before the pursuing Brown Shirts emerged from the alley. A corporal in charge of a detail of ten men was crossing the street here at the double-quick, hastening toward the scene of the riot.

Jimmy kept his eyes on Fritz Koller, and drew the corporal aside, whispering to him for a moment. The corporal nodded his quick understanding, and led the patrol around the corner at a lope. In a moment, Jimmy Christopher had the satisfaction of hearing the pursuing Brown Shirts firmly challenged by the patrol. That would stop them, and Jimmy was free to take his man to headquarters.

The streets were alive with people now, all running toward the waterfront. From the direction of the docks, they began to hear scattered shots. Apparently, the rioters, driven away from the warehouses, were bent upon venting their rage upon other portions of the city. No doubt there were other Brown Shirt *provocateurs* among them, who were working to keep them aroused. Many innocent men would be injured, perhaps killed, before the day was over. And this man, Koller, was one of those responsible for it.

Jimmy pushed the man through the crowds that were gathering, and headed toward Intelligence headquarters in the General Post Office Building. Koller realized where they were going, and he turned desperately to Jimmy. He wet his lips, wriggled to loosen the collar which was taut under Jimmy's powerful fingers, and said, "Listen, why can't we talk this over? Give me a chance, and I'll show you how it'll be worth your while not to take me in to headquarters." He was hopeful.

JIMMY SLOWED up. There was a gleam of triumph in his eyes. This was what he had hoped for. The charge of inciting to riot was punishable by death, and he had gambled that Koller would weaken and try to talk himself out of arrest.

"Well?" he asked uncompromisingly.

Koller wet his lips again, glanced around the street. "You've heard of the Brown Guards, haven't you?"

"Of course I have. But I don't believe the stories I hear. They say that you fellows who wear brown shirts with that hawk emblem belong to an organization known as the Brown Guards. But you've all denied it. I don't think it's true."

Koller studied him through lowered lids. "What if I were to tell you that it *is* true? What if I were to tell you that there is an

OPERATOR 5

JIMMY CHRISTOPHER

organization of Brown Guards? What if I were to tell you that we're so well entrenched that it's too late to do anything about us, and that in another week the country will be ours?"

Jimmy let his grip on Koller's collar relax. He appeared to be thoughtful, though in reality he was watching the other as a cat watches a mouse. "Who's your leader?" he asked.

Koller grinned. "Not so fast, my friend. But listen to me. You're one of President Sheridan's secret agents. You should know how powerful we're getting. You've seen riot after riot. You've seen a lot of Sheridan's plans crippled before they could develop. You've seen hundreds of brown shirts in the streets.

OPERATOR 5

Believe me, in a week the Brown Guards will be on top. Then we'll start cleaning up. Men like you, who worked under Sheridan, will be the first to go. You'll be stood against a wall—or worse."

Koller was talking swiftly, insinuatingly now. "You're no fool. Why don't you protect yourself? You play with me, give me a break, and I'll give you one when we come into power. You can straddle the fence, and save your own hide!"

Jimmy Christopher was seething inwardly. It was eloquent testimony to the short-sightedness of this Brown Shirt, that he should entertain the thought that a man like Operator 5 would allow the consideration of personal safety or benefit to stand in the way of the nation's well-being. But he gave no sign of his indignation.

Instead, he gave the appearance of being hesitant. Inwardly, he was jubilant. He had suspected all along that the Brown Shirt movement was a manifestation of some ambitious brain plotting to seize the dictatorship of America during these troubled times. Here he had verification of his suspicions. Outwardly, he seemed to be half-convinced.

"How do I know you're so strong?" he demanded. "Who's your leader?"

Koller said, "I can't tell you now. But if you'll let me go, I guarantee that someone will get in touch with you by tomorrow, and introduce you to the proper parties. It's worth a chance, isn't it?"

Jimmy eyed the other keenly. "Why are you so anxious not to be taken in? If you Brown Shirts are so powerful, you should have nothing to fear."

REVOLT OF THE DEVIL MEN

Koller's eyes became shifty. "Well, I've got a lot of things to do. I don't want to be locked up, even for a day—"

Jimmy broke in sharply, "Is it because you're carrying some papers—or some secret identification—that you don't want found?"

He saw the other start perceptibly, and knew that he had guessed correctly. He smiled tightly. "All right, Koller—let's go."

The prisoner snarled, but offered no physical resistance as Jimmy urged him toward the Post Office Building. Koller must have sensed that his captor had only been playing with him, for now he became silent, not making any further effort to win Jimmy over.

AT HEADQUARTERS, Koller continued his policy of silence. He merely sat in the chair into which Jimmy had thrust him, and refused to open his mouth. But when Jimmy ordered him to stand up to be searched, he sprang to his feet, furiously, and leaped at Operator 5 with murderous desperation. They were alone in Jimmy's office, and Koller had a chance, if he could dispose of Jimmy, to walk out of the building without being questioned.

The Brown Shirt's powerful arms flailed out at Operator 5, smashing blow after blow at him, in an effort to knock him out before he could draw the automatic which he had returned to its shoulder holster.

Operator 5 made no effort to get at his gun. He met the furious rush with the skilled science of the trained boxer. Operator 5 had learned all the tricks of the trade in the hard school of the

Intelligence Service, and there was nothing in the line of rough-and-tumble fighting that he did not know.

He blocked a hard left jab, and stepped back swiftly in time to avoid by a fraction of an inch a vicious knee aimed at his groin. For the moment Koller was off balance, and Jimmy sent his right fist traveling in a short, eight-inch, catapultlike blow that caught Koller on the side of the jaw with a thud.

The man's breath went out of him in a gasp, and his head snapped back with a sound like the crack of a whip. His knees buckled, and he collapsed slowly, unconscious, before he hit the floor.

Jimmy Christopher massaged his knuckles for an instant, then knelt beside the unconscious man and went quickly through Koller's pockets. He found cards and papers identifying him as Fritz Koller, and giving his residence as the City of Yonkers. Yonkers, twenty miles north of New York, was being rebuilt under the auspices of a former rival of President Sheridan's for the Provisional Presidency—a politician named Frederick Blaintree.

Jimmy studied those papers thoughtfully, wondering whether there was any connection between Blaintree and the Brown Guards. He found a small memorandum book in which hundreds of words and phrases were written in a small, careful hand, with numerals after each word. It was a code of some kind, and Jimmy pocketed it for further examination.

The only other thing of interest among Koller's effects was a silver chain on his key ring. The chain, itself, was not important, except for the fact that at one end of it there dangled a small charm such as one might have bought in the five-and-ten cent stores in the days before the Purple War. The charm was made of pressed gold, and was in the shape of a hawk. It was a duplicate of the figure embroidered on the sleeve-band of the Brown Shirts.

While Jimmy was examining this object, the phone on his desk rang. He started at the sound, for he was not used to *it* yet. For two years there had been no telephones in America. The devastating progress of the Purple Armies had destroyed every source of power, smashing into ruins the telephone central offices, and tearing down thousands of miles of telephone line.

They had been successful in reestablishing telephone service in some of the eastern cities. After two years of communicating by courier, heliograph and smoke signal, the jangle of the telephone was almost startling.

Operator 5 picked up the phone.

It was Tim Donovan at the other end of the line. "The riot's under control, Jimmy. Diane came back with me. Can we come up?"

"Come right up," he told the boy. "I've got a job for you and Diane."

A couple of minutes later, Tim Donovan and Diane Elliot were sitting in Jimmy's office, looking at the prostrate form of Fritz Koller.

DIANE ELLIOT'S face was flushed with the excitement of the last half-hour, and Jimmy thought that she looked more beautiful than ever. For an instant he felt a pang of remorse, because he was going to send her on a dangerous mission, and she was going to be exposed to unknown peril. But he smothered that thought. True, it had been hard for him at first, to bring himself to allow Diane to share in his adventures. He had balked at the idea that beauty such as hers might be extinguished by a bullet, or that she might meet a cruel death at the hands of the ruthless troops of the Purple Emperor.

But Diane Elliot had, herself, stifled that objection at the very outset, by flatly refusing to be left out their work.

"Where you go, I go, Jimmy!" she had told him unequivocally. "Try to stop me!"

He had never been able to stop her. Gradually, he had accepted the fact that her loyalty and love for him made her an invaluable aid. He made use of her more and more, and, as time went on and she showed that she knew how to take care of herself in tight spots, his worry for her had dwindled.

Tim Donovan wrinkled his pug nose at the unconscious figure of Koller. "That's the guy that was urging the mob on, back at the warehouses," he said. "Did you get anything out of him?"

Jimmy Christopher nodded. "Yes. I think I've got a hint as to the headquarters of the Brown Shirts. I'm pretty certain that there is an organization known as the Brown Guards. That's what I want you and Diane for."

He paused, then went on. "If my suspicions are correct, it's going to be a dangerous job for you two. I want you to go up to Yonkers, and scout around. If Blaintree is behind the Brown Guards, and if he's running that gang of revolutionaries from Yonkers, then you'll be walking into a trap. It'll be up to you to let me know what you've found."

REVOLT OF THE DEVIL MEN

Diane nodded, slowly. "I think you're on the right track, Jimmy. Tim and I will start tonight."

"Good. I'm going to see the President now, and report to him. I'll be back before you're ready to leave."

HE ESCORTED them out, then summoned a guard to remove Koller to a detention room. Finally, he made his way along the corridor toward the north wing, where President Sheridan's quarters were located.

On the way, he was greeted by dozens of officers and administrators attached to the government departments which functioned in the Post Office Building. He saw General Ferrara standing before the bulletin board in the main lobby, and joined him. Ferrara pointed to the news item which had just recently been posted there.

These bulletin boards had largely taken the place formerly occupied by newspapers for the dissemination of news to the populace. With the advent of the Purple hordes two years ago, almost all newspapers had been compelled to cease publication, as the means of communication were destroyed by the invading armies. Now, with the pressure of reconstruction so great that men worked day and night, there were far more important things than newspapers to print, and public bulletin boards were used in their place.

In every city and town that was being resettled by Americans, such a bulletin board occupied a prominent place in the public square, and news as it came over the newly installed telephone system, and by steamer from Europe, was at once posted.

OPERATOR 5

The item which General Ferrara indicated to Jimmy Christopher was a dispatch from London—

PURPLE EMPIRE BREAKING UP. FRANCE, SPAIN, ITALY AND ENGLAND ALREADY SECEDED FROM EMPIRE. RUSSIA, GERMANY AND BALKAN COUNTRIES EXPECTED TO FOLLOW. DEFEAT OF PURPLE ARMIES IN AMERICA AND DEATH OF EMPEROR RUDOLPH ARE UNDERLYING CAUSES. MOVEMENT CURRENT IN LONDON TO RECALL HOUSE OF WINDSOR TO THE THRONE AND TO ATTEMPT TO RECONSTRUCT THE FORMER BRITISH EMPIRE. GREAT PORTION OF PURPLE FLEET REVERTING TO ENGLAND. FEAR IS FELT THAT A GENERAL REIGN OF ANARCHY WILL GROW IN EUROPE AND ASIA UNLESS DEMOCRATIC GOVERNMENTS ARE ONCE MORE ESTABLISHED CONTROLLING POWERFUL NAVIES. ENGLAND TO SEND AN ACCREDITED AMBASSADOR TO UNITED STATES TO DISCUSS COOPERATION WITH AMERICA TO COMBAT ANARCHY.

The item which General Ferrara indicated to Jimmy Christopher was a local news bulletin—

BROWN SHIRT RIOTS EVERYWHERE IN CITY. RIOTS ALSO REPORTED FROM PHILADELPHIA, CAMDEN, BALTIMORE, AND AT NORFOLK SHIPYARDS. TELEPHONE COMMUNICATION WITH

NEW ENGLAND HAS BEEN CUT. BROWN SHIRTS REPORTED GATHERING AT GRANT'S TOMB IN LARGE NUMBERS AND WELL ARMED. FREDERICK BLAINTREE HAS ISSUED A STATEMENT THAT BROWN SHIRT DEMANDS ARE REASONABLE AND SHOULD BE GRANTED BY PRESIDENT SHERIDAN. HE STATES THAT IF HE WERE PRESIDENT THERE WOULD BE ENOUGH FOOD FOR ALL.

General Ferrara's fists clenched, and his face grew purple. "I tell you, Operator 5, it's Blaintree that's behind them all right. He's kept in the background all this time, and now that he figures the time is ripe, he's making his move!"

Ferrara was the commandant of the New York garrison, charged with the administration of martial law in New York. He fingered the butt of his revolver. "I'm going to take out a detail of men and personally place Blaintree under arrest!" he exclaimed.

Jimmy smiled tightly. "I'm afraid it's not as simple as that, Ferrara. If Blaintree has really been the brains behind the Brown Shirts—and this statement of his fairly proves it—then he's hoping you'll arrest him. Don't you see—that'll make a martyr of him, and will attract many men to his cause."

Ferrara sighed. "I'm afraid you're right, Operator 5. But what'll we do then?"

Jimmy shrugged. "Keep your men out all night. Suppress the riots with as little show of force as possible. Communicate with the commandants of the other cities and ask them to do the same. I'm working on a lead that may bring us something pretty soon. In the meantime, we'll have to sit tight and avoid playing into Blaintree's hands."

CHAPTER 3
THE GATHERING OF
THE WHIRLWIND

IT WAS a week later that Jimmy Christopher again visited the President's office in answer to an urgent summons. When he reached President Sheridan he found the nation's Chief Executive buried to the ears in work. There were executive orders to sign, a diplomatic agent from Great Britain just leaving, and half a dozen minor officials waiting for important decisions.

President Sheridan waved them all out, when Operator 5 entered.

Hank Sheridan was a thin, kindly-eyed man. He showed the strain of the last two years of warfare, during which the responsibility of a nation had lain heavily upon his shoulders. Now that strain was growing greater with every passing minute. His face had gathered new wrinkles, and there was a tired twist to his mouth that had not been there before.

But he hid all signs of weariness from Operator 5 as he worked over the huge mass of papers on his desk—papers embodying reconstruction projects affecting eighteen states, and thirty million people. As yet, telephone and railroad communication had not been completed with the Southern and Western states. There, famine and disease still throttled the great masses

REVOLT OF THE DEVIL MEN

of the population. It was about this that President Sheridan was talking to Operator 5.

"We have the Eastern seaboard well on the way to reconstruction, Jimmy," he was saying. "But what about the West and the Southwest? Someone has to undertake the job of carrying civilization out there again. We're getting daily messages by beacon signal and heliograph. Disease is spreading. Their crops are failing. Here in the East, we have the facilities for saving them. But we've no railroads, and no decent auto roads by which to bring them aid."

Operator 5 nodded, his eyes fixed upon a huge wall map behind President Sheridan's desk. On that map, there were hundreds of small red pins, mostly in the Southwest, denoting the spots from which desperate pleas for help had come in within the last week.

"I'd like to take that job, Hank," said Operator 5. "It would mean a twelvemonth trip, with a huge caravan of wagons. I'd have to take along physicians, and scientists, and food supplies and medicine, and hospital units."

President Sheridan looked up eagerly. "Then you'll go, Jimmy?"

Operator 5 hesitated. "There's one thing I'm worried about, Hank."

He paused a moment, and President Sheridan's eyes narrowed slowly. "You're thinking—there may be trouble here in New York while you're away?"

"That's right, Hank. We've got the populace on strict rations. It's necessary, and most of the people understand that if we don't use the ration system, we'll all starve in three months. But it's this secret propaganda going around, that's stirring the people up. I'm afraid something big is brewing—something that may topple all our work!" His face was grim now.

President Sheridan sighed deeply. "I don't like to say it, Jimmy. I've been worried about the same thing. That riot in Union Square two weeks ago; the sabotaging of the Kensico Reservoir last week; and the attack on the warehouses. They all point to an organized group. But who could be behind it? The country is pretty solid today—as it has never been in its history. Everybody realizes that we've got to pull together or perish. Who would be mad enough to stir up trouble—"

"I'm not sure," Jimmy Christopher interrupted, "but I have an idea. It isn't a nice idea. But asked Diane Elliot and Tim Donovan to go out and investigate it. You remember that when you were elected Provisional President by the Second Continental Congress in Chicago, your election was bitterly contested by a faction that wanted to elect Frederick Blaintree instead of you?"

The President's face grew suddenly tense. His eyes narrowed. "Blaintree! Jimmy, you can't mean that Blaintree is trying to foment trouble now! True, he's a politician. But politicians of his kind don't try to stir up revolution. Good God, Jimmy—if what you say is true, it means that Blaintree is a scoundrel!"

"I'm afraid that's what he is, Hank."

"What proof have you got? You say you sent Diane Elliot and Tim Donovan to investigate. Have they reported?"

"No, Hank. I sent them up to the colony that Blaintree has begun up in Yonkers. You gave Blaintree a charter to colonize

REVOLT OF THE DEVIL MEN

the ruins of Yonkers, on the site of the old city that the Purple Armies destroyed—"

"Yes, yes—of course. But what was their report?"

Operator 5 paused a moment, then said slowly, "They haven't reported yet, Hank. I haven't heard from them since they left!" His expression was worried, uncertain.

Sheridan's knuckles suddenly whitened on the desk, as he clenched his fists. He started to speak, then stopped, his eyes fixed on those of Operator 5.

Jimmy Christopher leaned forward, speaking tightly. "Diane and Tim left three days ago. They're no fools, and know how to take care of themselves. Their silence means only one thing, Hank—*that somebody has silenced them!*"

Operator 5's eyes were blazing. "If Blaintree has done anything to Diane and Tim, I'll throttle him with my own hands. Both of them worked with me all through the Purple War, and you know as well as I do, Hank, that I'd never have been able to bring about the death of the Purple Emperor, if it hadn't been for their loyalty. It would be pretty ironic, wouldn't it, if a rat like Blaintree were to be the cause of their deaths after what they've been through!"

Hank Sheridan arose slowly. "I hate to think that you're right in your suspicions, Jimmy. Blaintree is powerful, and he has a wide following. If he's planning to grab power, it will mean a disastrous civil war, and the ruin of everything we've been able to accomplish."

OPERATOR 5

Operator 5 nodded. "I'm going to find out definitely. I'm going up to Yonkers tonight."

"You can't do that, Jimmy. You've got this other job to do. I've prepared a caravan to leave tonight, for the Southwest. There are five hundred wagons, and three hundred riflemen, with huge supplies, all waiting to start. You're to take charge of it. A day's delay will mean the disrupting of that whole caravan—"

"But what about Tim and Diane?"

"Leave that to me, Jimmy. I'll send a squad of picked men up to Yonkers. I'll get to the bottom of this business. But you've got to start tonight. That's an order, Jimmy!"

Operator 5 hesitated. "Diane Elliot and Tim Donovan know that I've never left them in the lurch. If they're in trouble, they'll be expecting me to be on hand—"

"If they're in trouble, Jimmy, they'll get plenty of help!" President Sheridan said sternly. "The caravan is more important now. There are millions of people starving in the Southwest, and other millions dying of disease. Every minute of delay will mean more deaths. Your duty is with that caravan. And I give you my word of honor that Tim and Diane will be amply protected, or, if anything has happened to them, that Blaintree shall be well and amply punished!"

Operator 5's lips were tightly drawn. "All right, Hank, I'll accept your word for that. I'll start with the caravan tonight!"

President Sheridan smiled. "Good boy, Jimmy. I knew I could count on you!"

The two men shook hands.

An hour later, the great caravan, under the leadership of

Operator 5, was crossing the North River on the first leg of its historic trek toward the desolated lands of the Southwest.

CHAPTER 4
THE FATE OF A SPY

AT THE same time that Operator 5's great caravan was starting out from New York, a strange and disturbing scene was taking place in the reconstructed city of Yonkers, some twenty miles to the north.

Further east, on the road to the Kensico Reservoir, attempts had already been made to colonize parts of Westchester by those men who were employed upon the reconstruction of the reservoir, which was vital to the health and existence of New York. But here in Yonkers, there were but a few homes, of those who were sorrowfully returning to the place where they had been born and had lived.

It was strange therefore, that in spite of the sparse population of Yonkers, there should be so much activity in the grounds of the old Empire City Race Track, on the edge of town. A hundred torches illuminated the scene silhouetting the figures of almost two thousand men parading before the grandstand where formerly the judges of the Racing Association had been wont to gather.

These men marched in military formation, and each carried a rifle. All were attired in the same type of brown shirt which Operator 5 had seen upon the fomenters of trouble in New York

OPERATOR 5

City, and the numerous squad leaders carried white banners upon which there appeared the likeness of a black hawk.

Four men stood in the reviewing stand, saluting each time that one of the banners passed. The stand was in comparative darkness, lit only by two torch bearers who stood behind the group of four. This was no ordinary review of the armed forces of the nation. Rather, there was something furtive, something sinister about the whole proceeding that communicated itself to the marching men.

That air of secretiveness was emphasized by the elaborate precautions that had apparently been taken to keep the affair from being observed. There were armed men stationed as sentries at every gate of the grounds. In addition, several patrols covered every road leading to the race track. These patrols were mounted as well as on foot, and carried their rifles with a strange nervous tautness suspicious in itself. Several times, while that parade was in progress, the patrols fired their guns. Their orders were to make sure that no one approached close enough to observe what was going on—and, if anyone did manage to get within eyewitness distance, he must not be permitted to leave there alive. For this reason, the patrols fired whenever they thought they saw the movement of a human being.

However, in spite of all these precautions, two people *were* watching these proceedings with intent interest. These two were snugly ensconced in the wide space directly beneath the reviewing stand upon which stood the four officials.

That space extended back along the entire width of the stand,

REVOLT OF THE DEVIL MEN

The Brown Shirt officer slipped his arm around Diane's waist.

to the rear fence, and there was a small door there, overlooked by the numerous patrols.

One of the two observers was a young woman with chestnut hair and a soft white skin whose whiteness was enhanced by the khaki shirt she wore. The other was a pug-nosed, freckle-faced boy hardly out of his teens. From where they crouched, they could peer upward through a crack in the planks of the platform, and see and hear everything that went on upon the reviewing stand.

When they had entered the precincts of the city of Yonkers, a week ago, they had found every road patrolled, and a mysterious hum of activity about the race track. It had not taken Tim long to find this nook under the reviewing stand. They had secreted themselves here two hours ago, and, though they had no idea how to get away afterward, they were learning much now. Having fought through the entire war at the side of Operator 5, and sharing the perils of combat and espionage with him, they were hardly novices at this game. They were supremely confident that they would be able, in some fashion, to make their way through the cordon of Brown Guards with the information now being gleaned.

DIANE WAS crouching low, a notebook and pencil in her hand, while Tim peered upward through the crack. The four men had just mounted the platform, and Tim was saying in a whisper that just barely reached her, "It's Blaintree, all right, Di. He's the second one from the left. The first one is Doctor Oliver. You remember him; he was president of Stebbins University before the war. He used to write articles praising the Fascist governments of Europe, and claiming that we ought to have a dictatorship over here."

Diane Elliot nodded. "I remember him, Tim. I interviewed him once, and he tried to kiss me. I see that little mustache of his is as well trimmed as it always was."

Tim threw her a quick side-glance. "Did you smack him when he tried to kiss you, Di?" He was smiling when he said it.

"I certainly did. He threatened to have me fired from the Amalgamated Press, but then the War broke out." She made a few notes in her book. "Do you know the other two?"

"I know one of them—the one on the other end from Doctor Oliver. That's Senator Godkin—the fellow who wanted the country to start compulsory military training when he was in the Senate. But who's the fourth man—the one between Godkin and Blaintree?"

"That's Major Corvallo, or should I say, 'ex-Major Corvallo?'"

Tim Donovan's eyes flashed. "Of course! I never saw him, but I'll never forget the name. He's the chap that surrendered a whole brigade of the American troops to the enemy. He was deprived of his rank, and then he deserted." Tim paused, then went on. "What a gang, Di! Blaintree, defeated for the Presidency; Oliver, an out-and-out Fascist; Godkin, a reactionary of the worst sort; and Corvallo, a deserter! And they're banded together!"

Diane nodded bitterly. "Traitors all, Tim—and dangerous traitors at a time like this." Suddenly she tautened. "S-sh!" Blaintree was saying something to Corvallo. Every word would count now.

OPERATOR 5

REVOLT OF THE DEVIL MEN

OPERATOR 5

Diane's pencil raced as she transcribed what the Fascist leader was saying. There was very little light, but she wrote rapidly as she listened.

"Everything is set, Corvallo," Blaintree was saying. "I have another two thousand men in hiding across the Hudson, ready to join us."

Godkin, the man on the end, chimed in, "And I have four thousand men on Long Island. They've even better armed than these."

Blaintree spoke once more. "And there are three tanks that we salvaged from the war, hidden behind Fort Tryon Park, mounted with five-inch guns."

Diane Elliot was writing in the dark, in shorthand, as fast as they talked. Her lips tightened as she gathered the significance of the conversation.

Godkin was speaking now, but Tim and Diane lost most of what he said, because a brass band was passing in front of the reviewing stand at the moment. But Diane managed to write down this much now:

Men planted all over New York and the other key cities, provoking riots at every opportunity. Government... weakened. When Operator 5 leaves for southwest, we'll strike."

She said in a hushed voice, "Tim! This is worse than we suspected. They're well organized. They're planning perfectly. They—"

Tim squeezed her arm. More was coming.

It was Blaintree addressing Corvallo. "What do you think,

REVOLT OF THE DEVIL MEN

Major? Can you handle the thing with eight thousand well-armed men?"

"Certainly, Blaintree. There won't be that many armed government forces in New York. With the aid of the tanks, we'll overwhelm them. And once we capture or kill Sheridan, the other cities will fall, too. Then we'll announce that you've taken over the Presidency, and you'll dissolve the Congress. The country will be ours. With Operator 5 far away, there won't be a chance of failure!"

Diane uttered a low gasp. "Tim! We've got to get away from here. We've got to warn President Sheridan and Jimmy!" Tim Donovan laughed shortly. "It was fairly easy getting in past the patrols. But how're we going to get out? They've doubled the guards since we got in here." He paused.

"There are sentries everywhere, and the roads are patrolled. They're not taking any chances on the news of this leaking out before they're ready to strike."

Diane's hands were clenched. "But we have to get out just the same. We—"

"Wait!" Tim put a hand on her arm. It was Blaintree again. "You're to make sure there are no leaks, Major. Between now and the time we strike, no single person must leave Yonkers. Order your patrols to shoot on sight anyone who attempts to cross the city line!"

Tim grinned thinly in the darkness. "There's your answer, Di!"

The brown-shirted squads were marching out of the grounds now, and the attention of the sentries outside would no doubt be diverted toward the main gate. Tim now nudged Diane. "Now's the only chance we'll have. They'll have guards posted on all the roads later. Let's go!"

DIANE NODDED in the darkness, and crept toward the small gate at the back of the reviewing stand. They had left it unlatched, and Diane pushed it cautiously open, peered out. There was a sentry assigned to patrol this portion of the fence, but at the moment he was at the extreme end, watching the troops about to come out of the main gate.

Diane stooped low, pushed through the gate and raced for the shelter of a tree fifty feet away. Tim Donovan followed her quickly, after shutting the gate. They hugged the shelter of the tree's shadows, peering about for the safest direction in which to run.

The main road was a hundred yards away, and they could not hope to make it now. Tim said, "Wait here, Di. I'll climb up and look over the lay of the land."

He scrambled up the tree, while Diane waited below.

The sentry, apparently through watching the main gate, came back toward them. Diane moved carefully around to the far side of the tree from him. But she must have made some slight noise, for the Brown Shirt sentry swung around swiftly and leveled his rifle, peering into the darkness.

Diane remained rooted to the spot, crouching low against the tree. Tim remained where he was, hand on the revolver at his side. If the Brown Shirt decided to investigate, there was only one thing to do. This man was an American, just like Diane and himself, but he was also a traitor. Tim knew that if he had to, he

REVOLT OF THE DEVIL MEN

would shoot that sentry down just as he would shoot a foreign enemy of the country.

The Brown Shirt took a couple of steps forward, with his rifle cocked. "Who's there?" he called out.

Diane did not move. She was blended with the shadows around the tree. She, too, had her hand on her gun. It was true that there would be little chance of escape even if they did shoot this sentry, for there was another man on guard just around the corner of the fence, and there was a guard detail only a hundred feet down the other way, at the main gate. But neither Tim nor Diane had any thought of surrendering without a fight—not at all. The information they had just gathered was too important to be bottled up. They must make every effort, take every risk, to get it to President Sheridan and Operator 5.

The sentry came closer to the tree, evidently certain that someone was hiding there.

Diane, crouching on the ground at the foot of the tree, hoped that he would come close enough so that she could surprise him, get the drop on him. Their only hope was to overpower this sentry without giving the alarm to the rest of the Brown Shirts. But the sentry was too wary to fall into that trap. He remained at a respectful distance, and began to circle the tree. In a moment he would have a full view of Diane. That would be the end.

Suddenly, Diane knew what she had to do. She glanced up into the fork of the tree, and her eyes glinted as she noted that Tim was virtually invisible up there. Even if she were discovered and captured, Tim could remain free. If only the boy would refrain from coming to her assistance.

OPERATOR 5

She could easily have shot down the sentry now. But to do that would have brought the whole hornet's nest of Brown Shirts down upon them, and have insured their capture. She rose to her feet just as the sentry came around to her side of the tree. She kept her hand on her holstered gun, and called out, "Don't shoot."

The sentry grunted in satisfaction. "A woman, huh? You been here all the time? Come out an' let's take a look at you."

Diane heard a stirring in the fork of the tree above her, and she called out hurriedly, "No heroics, now. Hold everything!"

The words were meant for Tim Donovan, but the sentry misunderstood them. "What do you mean? Come on out and let's get a look at you!"

Diane stepped out from the shadow of the tree, and the sentry grinned. "A dame, huh? Come on over closer now!"

This man, Diane could see, was one of the rabble of criminals and underworld thugs who had cowered in hiding during the two years of the war, and who had come out only when all danger was past. It was these men who had formed guerrilla bands all over the country, and who were raiding, pillaging and stealing—hampering the reconstruction of the country by their criminal activities. Such men were naturally the nucleus of any force which traitors like Blaintree and Corvallo and the others would gather about themselves for an attempt to seize power.

Diane obeyed the man, and came to within three feet of him. He kept her carefully covered with his rifle, eyeing her slender figure, and noting the revolver at her belt.

"So you got a gun, eh? What you doing—spying on us?"

REVOLT OF THE DEVIL MEN

Diane said nothing. She was holding herself tense, hoping against hope that Tim would do nothing rash. If she allowed herself to be made a prisoner, Tim would have a chance to get away alone. He might be successful in getting back to New York with his message. If the boy could do that, it was all Diane asked. About her own fate she was indifferent—if only the President and Operator 5 could be warned of the danger which threatened. So she stood there under the sentry's leering gaze, and endured the lascivious touch of his eyes.

The Brown Shirt raised his voice and called out, "Ho, the guard! I've got a prisoner!"

In a moment a petty officer and two privates, all clad in the Brown Shirt uniforms, came dashing up from the detail at the main gate. The officer whistled when he saw Diane. "How did you get here?" he asked.

IT WAS plain that none of them recognized her as Diane Elliot, the friend and companion of Operator 5—for if they had they would not have wasted time questioning her, but would have taken her at once to their commanders.

"She's a spy!" the sentry told the officer. "She's been there all the time that the review was going on. I just spotted her when she moved. I guess she saw plenty, and was skipping to make her report!"

The officer looked at her speculatively. "Orders are to keep everybody away from here—and if any one does get to see what's going on, he's to be shot at once!"

Diane paled. "You mean—you're ordered to shoot without even a trial?"

"That's right, lady. Too bad it has to be a pretty girl like you. But what the hell—this is a dangerous business. We can't afford to take chances." He motioned to one of the privates. "Take her over to the fence. We'll give her a quick volley."

"But your superiors!" Diane protested. "Don't you have to get their permission to shoot a prisoner?"

The officer grinned. "No. Orders are to shoot anyone found here. But—he stepped closer to her, put a hand on her shoulder—"maybe if you was a nice kid, and wanted to make yourself agreeable, I could sort of forget orders." He turned and winked to the others. "What say, boys?"

The sentry and the two privates leered at Diane. "Sure. Be a nice kid!"

The Brown Shirt officer ran his hand down Diane's arm, slipped his arm around her waist. "Well—"

Diane's eyes blazed. She drove her fist into his face, and as he reeled back her hand darted to the gun in his holster. The sentry cursed and raised his rifle, and the officer, staggering backward, clawed for his revolver. In a moment a fusillade from the rifles of the sentry and the two privates would have riddled her body.

But before any one of them could pull a trigger, a heavy service revolver from the tree behind them roared and belched flame. The thundering shots reverberated in the night, smashing with deadly accuracy into the bodies of those Brown Shirts.

REVOLT OF THE DEVIL MEN

Once, twice, three times that gun roared, and the men with the rifles went hurtling back as if shoved by a great unseen hand.

Tim was firing from his fork in the tree—firing with vicious, angry accuracy, to kill.

The officer, who was standing slightly behind Diane, and therefore out of Tim's line of fire, was the only one left on his feet. His service revolver was out now, and he brought it down in a bead on Diane's breast. His face was contorted with rage, his finger contracting on the trigger. But before he could fire, Diane Elliot's own gun exploded once, squarely in his face, and his features seemed to disintegrate before her.

Diane took a single step backward, breathing hard, and in a moment she was joined by Tim Donovan, who had leaped down from his perch on the tree, the still smoking revolver in his hand.

Men were running from the direction of the main gate now, and shouts of alarm spreading all around them. The parading squads were streaming out from the gate after the guard detail. The whole neighborhood had been aroused by those shots.

The guard detail was the first to see Tim and Diane, with the bodies of the Brown Shirts at their feet, and they raised a great shout. Rifles sprang up, and lead began to patter about Tim and Diane, *pinging* into the tree behind them.

Tim shouted, "Let's go, Di!" He seized her hand, almost dragged her across the road toward a low-lying pile of ruins about a hundred feet away. There was shelter there, but no escape. However, it was better than nothing.

Diane gasped, "Tim! You shouldn't have shot at them. It was our only chance to get the news through. You should have let them do what they wanted with me. It would have left the way clear for you—"

Tim Donovan snorted. "And leave you to be manhandled by that scum? Nix, Di. Come on—we aren't licked yet!"

THEY REACHED the shelter of the ruins to the accompaniment of the staccato rattle of musketry behind them. Bullets shrieked and whined, screaming in the air close to their ears. They dropped, breathless, behind a pile of masonry, and both turned, emptying their guns at the nearest pursuers. They brought down three, and the others stopped for an instant.

In a crisis like this, both acted on instinct only. It was not necessary to give directions, or ask what to do next. They had been in just as tight spots many times before in their careers, and acted now without consultation. Both turned and ran, stooping low, in a line behind the masonry ruins, but parallel to the fence of the racing grounds. As they ran, they shoved fresh cartridges into their guns.

On the other side of the ruins they could hear an authoritative voice shouting, "Don't let them escape at any cost, men! Surround those ruins. Fix bayonets. Cover every inch of that masonry. Those two mustn't get out of here alive!"

"That's Corvallo!" Tim Donovan whispered to Diane. "He's taken command."

After that, neither said a word. Both were conserving their energy. They must get out of that pile of debris before it was completely surrounded, for once their escape from here was cut off, they would be smoked out with the bayonet. Even if they got out of the grimly closing circle, they would still face the greater task of evading the close net which the Brown Shirts would draw about the region of Yonkers. But their immediate concern was to get out of here now.

They ran for perhaps fifty yards, and could see the figures of the Brown Shirts closing in. Beyond the ruins, was the fence of the racing grounds. That way safety did not lie, for the squads of parading Brown Shirts were deploying out of there, lighting up all the surrounding grounds with their torches.

Backward, into the woods behind the ruins, there was a thin chance, for the Brown Shirts had not yet completed their encircling movement. But to reach those woods there was a cleared space of perhaps fifty yards which must be traversed.

Corvallo's men were no longer discharging their rifles, for there was danger now of hitting their fellows deploying on the other side of the ruins.

Tim and Diane crouched low, to keep from being seen above the jagged tops of the masonry. This mass of debris had once been a sumptuous dwelling place, occupied by some millionaire with sporting blood in his veins, who had wanted a residence near the track. The shellfire of the enemy troops had made a sickly wreckage of the grandiose buildings, and had torn down trees, rutted the grounds, and scorched the woods behind.

Diane glanced ahead, and glimpsed a small body of Brown Shirts coming around from the east. Soon they would be completely surrounded.

"We'll have to make a run for it, Tim," she said.

He nodded grimly. "Let's go, then!"

Both broke in a swift run, heading across the rutted grounds

OPERATOR 5

toward the shelter of the thickly growing, neglected woods. A shout went up from the Brown Shirts, and lead began to spatter about them. They ran low, clutching their guns tightly. Twenty feet, twenty-five… thirty….

They were almost at the fringe of the woods when Diane heard a little gasp from Tim at her side. She darted a swift glance at him, saw that he was stumbling.

"Tim!" the cry was torn from her throat. "You're hit!"

"It's—nothing, Di. Come—on!"

She seized his arm, steadied him.

The shouts behind him changed to yells of triumph as the Brown Shirts saw that one of the fugitives was hit. Lead came pumping after them thickly, but they had only a few feet more to go. Those few feet seemed like miles to Diane, for she felt Tim weakening under her grasp. The boy was running, with great spasmodic gasps, his face tightly set in a white, sweating mask.

At last they reached the fringe of the woods. In an instant they were among the trees, and the deadly drumming of the bullets became fainter. The shouts of the pursuers sounded in their ears yet. They would be in here after them, immediately. No time to rest, for Tim to catch his breath.

The lad stumbled along blindly, guided by Diane's arm. They fought their way through underbrush, pushing through twigs and branches that cut at their faces, stumbling, tripping, but keeping on.

They could hear the heavy feet of the Brown Shirts in the undergrowth behind them. Diane, looking back, could see the flares they were carrying blink through the trees, moving up toward them with menacing, inexorable threat. She heard Corvallo's voice raised in vindictive triumph: "Beat the woods, men! They can't escape now! The woods run down to the river, and there's no way for them to cross!"

DIANE PAUSED, still supporting Tim. The boy's knees were wobbly, and he turned a sweating face toward her. "Di! I—can't—go any farther. Go ahead. I'll hold them here." He grinned tightly. "I'll take a few of them with me. You double back. If I fight them here—it may attract their attention from—you!"

She shook her head violently, eyes brimming with tears. "Do you think I'd leave you, Timmy? Where are you hit?"

"It's—only my arm. My left arm. But—I guess I—can't take it…."

He slumped to his knees, resting against the thick trunk of a sycamore. "Go ahead, Di. I'll hold them."

They were closing in on them now. There was a man with a torch less than twenty feet away, and another on the other side of them, hardly fifteen feet distant. In a matter of minutes they would be discovered. Then the pack would come down on them, gleaming bayonets flashing in the torchlight, and that would be the end.

Diane looked about her desperately. They had no right to die here. They had a message of warning to carry to New York—a message that involved the safety of the whole country. There must be a way….

And suddenly Tim's young, eager, suddenly strong voice came to her in a fierce whisper. "Di! What's—that—over there?"

OPERATOR 5

He was pointing a wavering ringer through the surrounding blackness at a yawning hole in the ground, less than two feet from the tree against which he leaned.

Diane could barely distinguish his hand in the darkness, but she saw the direction in which he was pointing. The man with the torch on their right was coming closer, and he had been joined by two others.

As Diane crept past Tim to investigate the thing at which he was pointing, she could hear the vicious *swishing* sounds made by the bayonets of the Brown Shirts as they thrust into every dense mass of foliage passed.

Hastily, she crept over to the yawning hole, bent over it. Her hand, questing along its side, encountered the cold feel of metal. She thrilled. This was a shell hole, formed by the exploding shell from one of the huge guns of the imperial artillery during the war. But it was also more than a shell hole. She dropped into it, stretched out her hand, and found that the metal extended out past the side of the hole, in both directions. Bending down, she found that there was a metal floor!

"Tim!" she called in an urgent, exultant whisper. "Can you get over here? Quick!"

The boy crawled over toward her voice; literally fell into the shell hole. Diane caught him, eased his fall. She whispered into his ear, "Tim! This is part of the old aqueduct! The shell must have opened it. We can make our way along this!"

"Let's—go, then!" Tim Donovan seemed to have regained new strength at the prospect of escape. He managed, in spite of his wound, to help Diane pull dead leaves, and branches over the opening of the hole, to camouflage it against accidental discovery. Then they began to move cautiously along the tunnel of the old aqueduct.

They moved in utter darkness, feeling their way with a hand against the convex side. There was more than an inch of mud and water on the floor, and their feet slushed through it with difficulty. For a while they could hear the angry, baffled voices of the Brown Shirts, and then, as they progressed further into the tunnel, those voices died away.

After what seemed an interminable time, they stopped, and Diane clicked on her flashlight. Tim managed to get his jacket off, and she dressed the wound in his arm. The bullet had gone right through the flesh, and part of the muscle, and it was this which had been so painful. Tim sweated while she dressed the wound, but he essayed a grin when she finished. "What a baby I was! Only a flesh wound, but believe me, I almost keeled over from it!" He shook his head slowly.

There was a warm glow in Diane's eyes. "I know plenty of men who would have quit with a wound like that!"

At last he got his coat on again, and they headed farther into the tunnel. "I wonder where this'll take us out at?" Tim said.

Diane shrugged. "Wherever it leads us to, it's the road we've got to follow!"

And so they made their way in the utter blackness, through mud and slime, toward an end which they could not foresee....

OPERATOR 5

CHAPTER 5
MERCY'S FIGHTING CARAVAN

TWO HUNDRED and fifty miles southwest of Yonkers, the great relief caravan under the leadership of Operator 5 was already entering the beginning of its journey. It was making slow and painful progress, hampered by its own unwieldy bulk.

There were eighty huge covered wagons, each hauled by twenty horses, a hundred mounted riflemen, and a hundred and fifty doctors, nurses and scientists. That was the main column. In addition, there was a secondary column, which followed it, consisting of a herd of a thousand horses, and twenty additional wagons carrying fodder for the mounts and reserve food and ammunition for the main column.

Everything in those first eighty wagons was earmarked for relief of the stricken areas toward which they were marching. The secondary column was in the nature of a commissary and supply base. The herd of horses was brought up every night and yoked to the wagons, replacing the weary steeds that had dragged them during the day. In this way the horses were rested and fresh each day.

Of the hundred riflemen riding behind Jimmy Christopher, fifty were experienced hunters and trappers, whose job it was to forage for fresh food daily, thus relieving the drain upon the column's commissariat, Jimmy was dubious from the very beginning as to the success of the undertaking. Its very bulk, he felt, would defeat its purpose. But there was no denying the acute necessity for relief that existed, and this appeared to be the only way of bringing it.

The traveling was difficult, often impossible. The roads were rutted, pitted, destroyed by shellfire and by the movements of hundreds of thousands of troops and heavy artillery, which had traversed them many times during the two years of the Purple War. There were some stretches where there was literally no longer any road at all, and where the wagons careened dangerously on the brink of mountainsides, or narrowly escaped destruction in sweeping landslides of undermined rock.

Now the column was camped for the night outside of Harrisburg, Pennsylvania. Even here, so close to New York, there was misery and disease, and peril.

Emaciated women and children, and crippled men flocked out to them from the town, seeking relief from illness and wounds, and food. Jimmy had not expected to be compelled to break out the relief rations for many a day. But he had to start here. His heart sank as he thought of the many miles yet to be traversed by the caravan before it reached its ultimate goal in New Mexico. Ahead of him loomed the vast trail he had mapped out—past Harrisburg and across the Shenandoah Mountains, through the flooded coal mines of West Virginia and into the Cumberlands, thence southwestward across the flooded Tennessee River, around Reelfoot Lake and over the Mississippi. From here he would send small parties with a few wagons north toward St. Louis and south as far as they could get toward Vicksburg; while the main column continued on toward the Ozarks, past Tulsa and across the Arkansas into the

OPERATOR 5

old Santa Fe Trail, which had once before in our nation's history been traveled by covered wagons.

It was a two-thousand-mile trek. Farther on they would not be able to move faster than a walk—when the sun was hot, the horses weary, and the road nothing but a mess of mushed concrete. Then there would be stops at every small hamlet, town and city. There would be roving bands of raiders to repulse, outlaws to be chased, and there would have to be time for establishing governmental functions in cities and towns, and for delegating authority.

Six months? A year? Two years?

The way ahead looked long and tiresome, and filled with bitterness and sadness and weariness. Jimmy wished that he had Tim Donovan and Diane Elliot with him now, and for the long stretches ahead.

HE SIGHED, his eyes clouded with worry. He had let Tim and Diane go on a dangerous mission, and had not yet heard from them. Only Hank's insistence had prevailed upon him to leave without news of Tim and Diane. Perhaps they needed him.

A shudder went through him. A cold premonition of danger to them touched his heart. Always he had felt that way when peril threatened one of his little band. Was it because they were all so close to each other? Was it some form of telepathy—or was it just a hunch?

Whatever it was, Jimmy Christopher's mind was not on the

business of relief here in Harrisburg, but upon Tim and Diane—and the dangerous situation he had left behind in New York. Riots growing daily in violence—insidious murmurs spreading against Hank Sheridan's orders, against the shortage of food, against the idea of the caravan. Jimmy was sure trouble was lurking in the streets of New York. Whether it would come in a day or in a week or in a month, he did not know. He hoped only that Ferrara would be able to cope with the situation without bloodshed.

He maintained a continuous line of communication with New York by means of relay riders, and had set up signal beacon stations along the way.

BUT THE progress of the column became slower with each passing day from now on. They had set out in the early part of May, and late July found them camping at White Sulphur Springs in West Virginia. Two long months had told on the personnel of the caravan. Already they were weary—both physically and mentally, as well as spiritually.

Jimmy Christopher found that he was right in his predictions. Everywhere that they stopped, there arose petty bickering, and discontent. Jimmy's schedule had been knocked into a cocked hat. His hopes of reaching the Mississippi by early Fall were gone. This meant that those people living west of the Mississippi would starve anti-freeze in earnest when the cold weather set in.

And he was not so happy about the reports reaching him from New York. Hank Sheridan sent him regular messages by courier—messages that he dared not trust to the beacon stations for transmission. Senator Godkin was in New York,

OPERATOR 5

making violent speeches against the administration. And in accordance with the tenets of free speech, which the President was bent upon upholding, Godkin was being allowed a free hand. Thousands were listening to him, and as a result there were daily committees of workmen visiting the Post Office Building, demanding larger rations.

The Brown Shirts, too, were making dangerous progress. Their arm-band insignia could be seen all over the streets of New York these days, and they strutted about boldly, sneering at the hard-working officers of the Presidential staff. A large number of them had attended a speech of Godkin's at Union Square, in which the ex-Senator had openly charged that the ulterior purpose of Operator 5's caravan was to carve out an empire for himself in the southwest. Godkin's flowery oratory had carried the crowd off its feet. He told them that Operator 5 was taking away food which they, themselves, needed, in order to further his own ambitions, and the crowd had become so infuriated that they streamed toward the East River storehouses with the intention of sacking them.

Fortunately, General Ferrara had a company of loyal riflemen stationed there, and dispersed the mob with a few tear-gas bombs. But something was due to break at any moment, and Hank Sheridan wrote, in his letter, that he wished Operator 5 were back.

But the thing that worried Jimmy Christopher more than anything else was the news that no single word had yet come in from Diane Elliot or Tim Donovan. Hank Sheridan had sent a detail up to Yonkers to look for them, but the men had found no trace. This was disturbing news, but Jimmy had little time to brood over it. His hands were full, right here with the caravan.

In spite of the trouble he was encountering, he was able to accomplish one concrete thing that promised definite results. This was the opening of the two great oil refineries near Marietta, Ohio. He had purposely detoured the caravan in order to cover the oil-producing territory there, and had found the oil fields in fair condition. His technicians had been able to place them in production again, and, with only a few repairs, the refineries were once more set to work. This would now be a source of fuel for the many industries dependent upon petroleum in order to operate. It would also put into motion many thousands of automobiles now lying idle. Before he left Marietta, he had the satisfaction of seeing the first oil flowing into the pipe lines toward the refineries.

He did not know at that moment, that this accomplishment of his was to be one of the outstanding factors in the great disaster soon to befall the land.

Wearily, he pushed on, with his huge unwieldy caravan, farther south into Tennessee. Then suddenly, a month later, the couriers ceased to come through from New York.

There were routine messages on the beacon system, but no couriers. Jimmy sent several queries back on the beacons, and the answers he got were far from reassuring.

The first reply on the beacons came when they were at Nashville. Andy Bretton brought it in to him. Operator 5 read it, frowning—

OPERATOR 5

> Couriers have been leaving daily as usual. Cannot understand why they did not get through. They carried important messages. Will try again today. H.S.

Jimmy looked up at Bretton. "It's twelve days since we've had a courier from Hank," he said. "We've got to find out why they're not getting through."

Andy spread his hands. "How'll we find out?"

Jimmy stood up. "We'll send a man back along the route we've taken. We'll follow him up with another in an hour, and then with still another. It's important to find out at what point Hank's couriers are being stopped."

"I'll attend to it," Bretton said, and left.

The caravan moved on, and Jimmy waited for news from his messengers. He reasoned that if Hank's couriers were being stopped somewhere, his own men would also be stopped at the same place. He had warned them to be on the lookout for a trap, and hoped that they would be able to escape and return with a report. But to his surprise he received a beacon message two weeks later, that all three of his men had come through to New York, safely!

The caravan was within a few days' march of the Mississippi when that news came in, and they were well on into September. Jimmy was anxious to get across the big river before the cold weather set in, in earnest, and he pushed on—though he was really troubled about the mystery of Hank's messengers. He was trying to guess what important messages Hank could have sent him, which he dared not trust to the beacons. Was it revolution? Was it something about Tim and Diane?

REVOLT OF THE DEVIL MEN

HE SENSED the deadlines of the situation. Somewhere along the line, someone was deliberately stopping Hank's couriers, of course. And this someone was clever enough to let his own messengers through going east, thus not disclosing the point at which the break occurred. The danger was that this person might also get control of the beacon system at the same point, and thus cut off all communication between the caravan and New York.

Jimmy Christopher called a conference of all his sub-commanders in the caravan. To them he stated the situation.

"So you can see," he finished, "that there is the danger of our being entirely cut off from the East. That would mean that we'd be absolutely on our own. If an emergency arose, we'd have to face it ourselves, and not look for help to New York."

Andy Bretton raised his eyebrows. "What sort of emergency, Operator 5?"

Jimmy shrugged. "We're going into a territory where there hasn't been any law for two years. There are plenty of roving bands of raiders—and some of them are pretty strong. After all, we have only a hundred armed men. After we cross the Mississippi, we'll be in dangerous territory. From there on we may have to fight our way into New Mexico. If we should meet a superior force of raiders, and be besieged by them, we'd not be able to summon help. In addition to that, we'll probably have an enemy at our backs; because whoever is cutting our communications isn't doing it for fun."

He paused, and looked around the long, rough pine table

where the conference was taking place. "So what do you say, gentlemen? Before it's too late, do any of you want to turn back?"

There were ten men at that table, and they looked at each

REVOLT OF THE DEVIL MEN

other, expectantly. Not one of them offered to go back. Jimmy sighed, and his lips softened in a smile. These were all good men. There was Andy Bretton, and George Macklin, and Sam Baxter—all had fought through the Purple War. And there was Frank Simms, who had lost an eye at the Battle of the Continental Divide, but who glared fiercely out of his one remaining orb, as if challenging any of the others to say that he wanted to go back. There was Tobias Follings, whose wife and child had been executed by the enemy in Pittsburgh, and who had followed Jimmy Christopher in the historic raid when they had recaptured the Steel City from the enemy by sheer daring and courage. Toby Follings had run amok that day, wielding a bayonet until it broke in the body of one of the hated Imperial Troopers who had killed his wife and child.

The other men at that table were all equally tried and true. They would go to the end of the world with Operator 5, if necessary. Their glances told him as much.

Jimmy's smile tightened. "All right, then," he said. "We'll carry on. Forced marches from here, until we cross the Mississippi. From there on we'll consolidate the auxiliary column with the main caravan. It'll be too dangerous to be separated. We'll throw out scouts, too." He nodded to Andy Bretton. "You'll take care of all that Andy?"

Captain Bretton saluted. "As ordered, Operator 5," he said.

JIMMY WAITED till his juniors had all filed out. Then he wrote out a message to Hank Sheridan, and took it over to the beacon operator. As he crossed the encampment, he heard the neighing of horses, the low home-sick singing of the riders, and

OPERATOR 5

the crooning of several hundred Negroes who had gathered close to the great circle of covered wagons to wait for morning when the food would be handed out.

As it was wherever they stopped, word went out swiftly to all parts of the surrounding countryside that the caravan was here, and hungry people flocked to it from everywhere. It was no use to announce that the caravan itself was not dispensing food to individuals. They were hungry and wanted to be fed. The usual procedure was to turn over a full wagon load to the local authorities, who would then set up rationing bureaus, and appoint clerks to dispense the food. Jimmy's caravan did not have the facilities to do this work, for the men were all dog-tired from the day's journey, and hungry themselves. But invariably the sight of the hundreds of starving persons who flocked to them, too impatient to wait for the morning, was too much for the members of the caravan, and they had gotten into the habit of taking turns at giving out food to those who asked for it. Four or five men each night were assigned to this task, and now those Negroes out there in the night were singing joyfully over the stew they were cooking out of the cans.

A hundred campfires were burning within the circle of the covered wagons, and sentries were posted to keep all strangers out. Jimmy had made it a rule ever since Harrisburg that no one was to be allowed within the circle unless a member of the caravan, or unless possessing a pass.

The only member of the caravan who was outside the circle of covered wagons was the heliograph operator, who had taken up his position on a hill about two hundred feet from the encampment. The reason for this was so that the operator at the next town would be able to read his signals and not be confused by the camp-fires.

Jimmy made his way to the hill, and gave the man a message. "Send this through to Hank Sheridan fast," he ordered. Then he composed the message.

The operator, Larry Bridges, was a youngster who had seen service with the American Defense Force. He had been a second lieutenant in the signal corps, and had sat at a key, sending Morse Code, all through the first Battle of New York, when the waves of the Imperial Army had swept our defense force back in the first great attack of the invasion. He had stayed at that key, sending warnings to every part of the country, flashing orders to all the widely separated American troops. He had remained at the key a few moments too long, and been taken prisoner, sent into the labor battalions around Pittsburgh, from which he was rescued when Operator 5 staged his daring raid on that city. He was as devoted to Jimmy Christopher as any of Operator 5's more intimate companions—and, what was more, no one could send code so fast.

"Do you remember Code Fourteen, that we used during the war, Larry?" Jimmy asked him.

Larry Bridges nodded. "I'll say I do, Operator 5. I've been practicing it in my spare time."

"Good. Do you think Hank Sheridan has a copy of Code Fourteen?"

"He has. I remember seeing it on his desk one day."

OPERATOR 5

"Then send this message in that code. I'll help you to encipher it."

He sat down opposite Larry, leaning over the make-shift table which the young second lieutenant had set up, and they worked from memory for twenty minutes. At last, they had the message enciphered. The advantage of using Code Fourteen was that it could be disguised to read as a simple message, and yet hide its true meaning. Jimmy hoped that Hank Sheridan would recognize that it was coded. The message hidden in the communication read—

> Your couriers are not coming through. I am afraid our beacon messages; will be cut next Tell me what is happening in New York. Use code fourteen.
> Operator 5

JIMMY CHRISTOPHER left Larry Bridges to send the message on the heliograph, and got a mount to ride into Union City to confer with the mayor about setting up relief and food stations. There would be small sleep for Operator 5 tonight. In fact, he got very little sleep, for he had to take care of all the arrangements wherever the caravan stopped. Since they traveled all day, these matters had to be attended to at night. He slept mornings, in one of the wagons, after the caravan got under way.

Andy Bretton met him as he was leaving the circle of wagons, and swung his horse in alongside. "I think I'll ride in with you tonight, Operator 5, if you don't mind."

Jimmy raised his eyebrows. "You'll miss a lot of sleep, Andy."

"That's all right, sir. But I'll feel a lot better if I know you're not alone tonight. I've been hearing talk around the encampment this evening, since the conference. I heard one fellow say that if something happened to Operator 5, the whole caravan would be sidetracked here, and they'd have plenty of food to last for months. I don't like the way the chap said it."

Jimmy smiled. "You think I'll be bushwhacked?"

"I don't know, sir, but I'd like to be along in case anything should happen." Significantly, Andy Bretton lifted the Springfield from the sheath alongside his saddle, and swung it under his arm. "This is a good gun, sir. It's one of the few left with telescopic sights—and I'm a marksman."

Operator 5's eyes were kindly in the darkness. "I hope you don't have to use it, Andy. We have enough trouble without any extra shooting." He changed the subject. "What was this man like—the one whom you heard talking outside?"

"He was a giant of a fellow, with a black beard and a shock of black hair. He looked as if he hadn't been washed for months. He was in a group just outside the encampment. There were half a dozen men there, and none of them looked any better than he did. They got their rations, and built a fire out there. They didn't think they were talking loud enough to be heard, but the wind was coming my way, and I caught what this man with the beard said. Then I heard one of the others call him Cutler, and that was all I could get—"

"Cutler!" Jimmy Christopher exclaimed. "Are you sure?"

Andy nodded. "Pretty sure, sir. Do you know him?"

Jimmy laughed shortly. "If it's the Cutler I've heard of, then I'm afraid we're going to have trouble. Jock Cutler—he's the

OPERATOR 5

leader of a guerrilla band that's been raiding through here for months. That whole crowd came from one of the state prisons near here. There were about twenty of them in the original group. They were released, together with all the other convicts who offered to serve in the American Defense Force, but Cutler and those twenty or so went their own way. They deserted the day after being released, and they've been raiding and killing ever since!"

Andy Bretton whistled. "If I'd only known that! Of course I've heard of Jock Cutler, but I never connected the name. He came in so boldly, that I never suspected it was the same man—"

They had pushed their horses around a bend in the road, and now the murky Mississippi was visible, with the few lights of the newly built Union City straight ahead. The horses picked their way carefully along the road, avoiding the ruts and places where the concrete was cracked into fissures almost a foot in width.

On their left there was a stretch of marshy land, and on their right a thickly wooded copse ran down at right angles from the road to the river.

IT WAS from this copse that the first shot came. There was the crash of a shot, the whine of a bullet. Jimmy Christopher and Andy Bretton, both old campaigners, acted instinctively. They swung low on their saddles, toward the side away from the woods. The bullet screamed harmlessly over their heads. It had been aimed too high, anyway.

But the next might be closer. Andy yelled, "Let's turn and ride back—"

"No!" Jimmy shouted. "They've got the road covered behind

REVOLT OF THE DEVIL MEN

us. Ride ahead!" It was true enough. Jimmy Christopher had thrown one quick glance to the rear, and seen the group of riders coming out into the road a hundred feet back. He kicked Andy's horse, spurred his own, and the two raced ahead toward the river. They rode low, resting almost on their faces, while more shots pursued them. In a moment, another group of riders appeared ahead.

Jimmy Christopher's lips tightened. This was a perfect trap. He had no doubt that these men intended to kill him, for they did not call out, or attempt to parley. They shot grimly, silently, spattering the road with lead.

Operator 5's service revolver was out, and Andy Bretton was already pumping shots from his Springfield at the men barring the road. One fell, and then another, and now they were close to that group. Firing from the woods bad ceased. The group in front spurred their horses out fanwise, so as to block the whole road and, at the same time, leave themselves free to fight.

Almost a dozen men were in this group, not counting the two whom Andy had shot. Andy's rifle was still barking, and now Operator 5 was close enough to use his revolver.

The raiders had also scored, for Jimmy caught the sudden lurch of Andy Bretton's horse, saw Andy go flying over the head of his mount, to land in the marsh at the left of the road.

Now Operator 5 was alone against these men, and he rode forward like a whirlwind, right into the teeth of the hail of lead. His gun roared and bucked in his hand, and he swung it around in a semicircle. He saw men go down before him, saw that he had made a hole in the circle in front of him. Into that hole he

OPERATOR 5

rode like a thunderbolt, his revolver empty. He hurled the useless gun at a face in front of him, took a bullet in his right forearm, and then he was through.

The raiders swung after him, yelling. Six of their number were down, but the others from the woods as well as those from down the road were spurring up to join them in the chase of this lone man.

Jimmy Christopher however, had no intention of running and leaving Andy Bretton here. He had caught sight of Andy, stumbling to his feet in the marsh, and staggering toward the road. Apparently it had been the horse who was hit, and not Bretton.

Jimmy Christopher whirled his own mount sharply, heading it toward the woods at the right. He glimpsed an opening between two tall trees, and urged his horse in there, just as the first of the riders swept past. Their own momentum carried them on for several yards, and, as they reined in, those behind piled up against them.

This caused a moment's confusion in their ranks. Operator 5 seized that opportunity to leap from his horse and dart backward through the woods until he reached the spot where the raiders had first ambushed them. On the road here, there lay two dead horses, one resting squarely upon the body of its rider. A little farther over there lay another dead raider, his rifle still at his side. Other bodies strewed the road for several feet in either direction.

OPERATOR 5 darted out, seized one of the rifles, and dropped to his knees behind a dead horse. He shouted to Andy Bretton, who was still weaving about blindly in the marsh, no doubt dazed from the shock of his fall. "Here, Andy! Quick!"

REVOLT OF THE DEVIL MEN

Bretton heard the call. It served to focus his mind and drive the haze from it. He dropped into a crouch, and ran toward where Jimmy had taken shelter behind the horse. The raiders, almost twenty feet beyond, had already begun to spur into the woods when they heard Jimmy's shout. They had thought that he was still in there among the trees, trying to escape. Their astonishment when they learned he had not run away was comical. For a moment they milled among themselves, before a gruff voice shouted, "Mount! Mount, you fools! Mount and charge them!"

Jimmy Christopher laughed tightly. He raised the rifle and carefully sighted. Then his finger contracted on the trigger, and he fired once, twice, three times. He stopped, just as Andy Bretton reached him and threw himself flat alongside of him. "Pick up a rifle, Andy! This is touch and go!"

Jimmy's first three shots had dropped three men. Now the others started to return his fire, shooting wildly, vindictively, to avenge their fellows. Jimmy put a hand on Andy Bretton's arm, kept him down while a hail of lead sang over their heads. Then he reached out and groped in the saddle-bags of the horse behind which he crouched. He found spare clips, and pulled them out. They fitted his rifle. He slipped one in, while Andy Bretton pumped his newly acquired gun at the horsemen. In a moment, Jimmy's gun was loaded, and he picked up with the barrage where Andy had left off to reload.

The continuous, accurate, deadly fire of these two men was too much for the grouped raiders. They broke and rode wildly toward the river, leaving half a dozen dead and wounded behind.

OPERATOR 5

With a *whoop*, Andy Bretton came running out from behind the barricade, and raced after them. Jimmy Christopher covered him with rifle fire directed against the retreating raiders.

Andy reached the fallen men. Two horses were nosing among the dead, and Andy seized their reins, led them back. In a moment the two men were mounted again. Andy said, "Do we go back, Operator 5?"

Jimmy Christopher looked at him, enigmatically. "Take a guess, Andy."

Andy grinned. "I guess we go forward!"

Jimmy nodded, smiled, and the two rode ahead side by side toward the river, after the fleeing raiders.

A groan reached their ears from among the wounded, and Jimmy dismounted while Andy sat his horse erect, watchful, lest the raiders return and surprise them.

Jimmy Christopher picked his way among the dead toward the sound of the groans. It was the bearded man whom Andy had described. Andy watched Jimmy stoop beside him, and called out, "Look out, Operator 5—that's Cutler!"

Jimmy nodded, and knelt beside the wounded man. He was wounded in two places. A bullet had caught him high up in the chest, on the left side, and there was also a great gout of blood on his shirt over the stomach. He pushed Jimmy's hand aside feebly.

"Won't—do no good. Operator 5. I'm—done. Going fast Jimmy didn't try to disillusion him. The man was hard. He had lived a hard life and he was dying the hard way. Jimmy merely said, "You're Cutler, aren't you?"

The bearded man nodded with an effort. "You're a good—

scrapper, Operator 5. We thought—we'd get—you. That would—finish the caravan."

"Why did you want to do that? What would it get you?"

Cutler's eyes were glazing fast. "That Doctor Oliver—he passed your column—it was him egged me on. He said—if we crippled the caravan—he'd arrange it for me to be made—governor of Louisiana when Blaintree—came into—power. Damn him!"

Jimmy's grip tightened on Cutler's shoulder. The man's head fell back; his jaw dropped. He was dead.

Slowly, Jimmy Christopher lowered him to the ground. He looked up to meet Andy Bretton's eyes. "Did you hear that, Andy? Doctor Oliver—in league with Blaintree? And he's way out here. It must be Oliver who's stirring up all this trouble along the road."

Andy Bretton nodded slowly. "I guess we got to get this Doctor Oliver, sir—if we want to finish the trek alive!"

"I think we will!" Operator 5 agreed with him.

CHAPTER 6
CITY OF THE DOOMED

IN NEW YORK CITY, President Sheridan was coping with a number of problems that threatened to engulf him by their very complexity. The riots which had been in their incipient

OPERATOR 5

stages when Operator 5 left three months ago were now occurring with greater frequency and viciousness. The Brown Shirts were openly agitating in the streets of the city for the violent seizure of food stores. Senator Godkin spoke every night in different sections, inflaming the thoughtless mob to discontent against the government. Several attacks had actually been staged against the food warehouses, and these had only been repelled by the prompt action of General Ferrara. Strikes were being called daily upon projects of vital importance to the continued survival of the nation.

President Sheridan had hoped to complete the major portion of the huge reconstruction program in New York City before the cold weather set in; but the strikes paralyzed him, and work was virtually at a standstill.

These were the things Hank Sheridan was writing to Jimmy Christopher by courier. There were other matters, however, which he did not tell Operator 5, for fear that Jimmy might forego the expedition to the Southwest, and return home. For instance, he did not inform him that a midnight raid upon the Kensico Reservoir had cut off New York's water supply, and that the city was now dependent upon that pumped from the ocean and distilled in two big plants erected hurriedly in Brooklyn. The Kensico Reservoir was the sole source of water supply for the entire city, since the other great water sheds had been destroyed by the Purple troops.

The raid took place one night, three weeks after Operator 5 had left with the caravan. The detail of guards on duty there had been surprised by a large party of horsemen who shot them down without warning, and then proceeded to open the sluice gates, allowing thousands of gallons of fresh water to run out and inundate the Westchester countryside.

The next morning, New York City found itself without water. The situation became acute. People stormed the Government House, demanding water. Thoughtlessly, they blamed Hank Sheridan for this trouble. That feeling was intensified by sly agents of the Brown Shirts, who circulated among the crowds and dropped a word here and there, to the effect that Sheridan should have taken greater precautions to guard the Kensico Dam. They did not tell the crowd that the captain in charge of the detail had been badly betrayed by Blaintree, who had entered the guard room to talk to him.

The captain, a young veteran of the Purple War by the name of Coles, entertained no suspicion of Blaintree, for he knew him only as a man active in political life, and one who had run for the Presidency of the United States. If he had any suspicions, they were lulled by Blaintree's geniality and assumed good fellowship.

But it was Blaintree who drew a gun and shot him in the back the moment he turned away. And it was Blaintree who then used the captain's signal whistle to summon the guards in from their posts around the reservoir.*

---

* AUTHOR'S NOTE: We have indisputable proof that Frederick Blaintree was the man responsible for this massacre. In spite of the fact that he was one of those who raised his voice loudest in criticism of Hank Sheridan for failing to take greater precautions to guard the reservoir, we know definitely now, that it was he who engineered the whole thing. In support of this charge we

OPERATOR 5

Corvallo shot Hank Sheridan down!

REVOLT OF THE DEVIL MEN

That whistle was used by Captain Coles when he wished to relieve the guard. He had two hundred men under his command here, and half of them generally stood guard duty while the other half went to their homes. When the men reported in for duty, Coles would sound his signal whistle, and the guard would come in to be relieved. This time, however, there was no relief for them.

When they were all assembled in the courtyard in front of the executive office, Blaintree's Brown Shirts, hidden in the office, let loose with machine guns, cutting the guard down mercilessly. And they did not cease their grim work until every one of those bewildered men was dead. They could not afford to leave a single one of them alive to tell the story.

The same procedure was repeated when the other hundred men reported in for duty an hour later. Two hundred men were slain in cold blood. It was the most detestable massacre in the

---

have the signed affidavits of five of the Brown Shirts who took part in the raid, who confessed and signed those affidavits on their death beds. In addition, we have an illuminating page from the diary of Diane. The raid took place during the time when she and Tim Donovan were prisoners of the Brown Shirts, and Diane records that Blaintree came into the room where she was confined and openly boasted of the massacre, telling her that it was a stroke of genius, and that it would aid in the gradual breaking down of the prestige of the government—which was, of course, the ultimate aim of the Brown Shirt conspirators. Diane records that Blaintree told her of these things in order to impress her with his own ruthlessness, so that she would realize the hopelessness of her own and Tim Donovan's positions, and agree to do the things he demanded of her.

history of our country. The bodies were carted away in the night, and buried in a ditch six miles from the reservoir, where they were not unearthed until almost two years later.

The Brown Shirts then opened the sluice gates of the dam, and rode away in their homes, while Blaintree, himself, hurried to New York to be on hand when the shortage of water was discovered in the morning.*

IT WAS only Hank Sheridan's quick thinking the next day, which prevented a large-scale riot by the inhabitants of New York, who were stricken with panic at the thought of being left without a drop of water. Sheridan remembered the two old breweries in Brooklyn which had been out of use for more than two years, and which he had been considering turning into chemical plants as soon as he could get the equipment.

He stepped out upon the broad steps of the Post Office Build-

---

* AUTHOR'S NOTE: It must be borne in mind that New York was not at this time a metropolis of six million people, but only of about a million and a half. The rest of the population of the city was scattered among the outlying sections of Connecticut and New Jersey and Massachusetts. Therefore, the Kensico Reservoir was sufficient to supply water for all the needs of New York. At this time Hank Sheridan had been considering plans for putting back into operation the water sheds at Croton as well as those farther up, in the Adirondacks, preparatory to taking care of the great influx of population which he expected to return to New York as soon as conditions became more settled. The raid on the Kensico Reservoir was a body blow to him, and it set back his plans for the reconstruction of the city by more than a year.

REVOLT OF THE DEVIL MEN

ing, and raised his hands in signal for the huge throng of shouting men and women to be quiet.

"I promise you water within twelve hours!" he shouted to the crowd. "You know me, and you know that I have never broken a promise yet. Now if you will go back to work, I'll see that every home in the city is supplied with water by tomorrow morning. We'll have some coming in tonight—and it'll be fresh, clean, water!"

Many in the crowd began to cheer the announcement. They knew that Hank Sheridan was a man of his word. They knew that he had given much in the service of the country, and that he would not fail them now.

But there were many *provocateurs* of the Brown Shirts among that crowd, and they began to shout and heckle Sheridan.

"Where you going to get the water?" one of them demanded. "Outa the ocean?"

Hank Sheridan pointed a dramatic finger at that man. "Yes!" he thundered. "I'll get it out of the ocean, and I'll distill it. And let's see if the Brown Shirts can dry up the ocean on us as they dried up the Kensico Reservoir!"

That retort caught the fancy of the crowd. Sympathy switched to Hank Sheridan. The grumblings of the Brown Shirt agents failed to stir them up now. The crowd dispersed, cheering Hank Sheridan, and men went back to work. Soon the word spread throughout the city that the President was taking care of the water supply, and the riots which had been starting all over town slowly quieted down.

BLAINTREE, OLIVER, and others of the Brown Shirt

OPERATOR 5

leaders watched the gradual subsidence of the trouble, and were disgruntled. They had failed to accomplish as much as they had hoped by their treachery. In the evening, when the two breweries, distilling thousands of tons of water, began to distribute it by horse-drawn carts all over the city, Blaintree saw that his bloody massacre had accomplished nothing. But he *had* accomplished this much—Hank Sheridan was forced to use a good deal of his precious supply of coal to keep those distilleries going, and also to open six more in Manhattan and the Bronx. The coal supply was very low, being conserved for necessary operations, such as the many factories which were being opened to produce clothing for the coming winter months. The coal was also needed for construction work in the city, as well as the building and repair of ships necessary for fishing and transportation.

Hank Sheridan did not write of this to Operator 5—and there were many other things in the ensuing months that he did not mention.

As the weeks hurried on into months, and there was still no word from Diane Elliot or Tim Donovan, Hank Sheridan grew more lean and gaunt. He hated his task of writing each day to Jimmy, for he must tell him again that he had not heard from those two. He had sent scouts into Yonkers and the surrounding territory, but had found nothing.

Blaintree had become more cautious after finding that Tim and Diane had penetrated his secret. He did not hold any more meetings or drills, in the Empire City Race Track grounds, but had his Brown Shirts drill surreptitiously at night, in far removed places, a company at a time. There were no more public mass meetings. The men whom Hank Sheridan sent into Yonkers found everything peaceful, and reported that there was apparently no trouble in Blaintree's district.

And this was exactly what the Brown Shirts wanted. After the fiasco of the Kensico massacre, they changed their policy, and worked more secretly, not flaunting their defiance of the government as openly as they had done in the past. They turned more and more to the use of sabotage. Fires broke out with alarming frequency on many of the public projects, damaging them and setting back the work of reconstruction by months. All the time they were recruiting more and more members, until by August they had numbered thirty thousand.

Doctor Oliver had set out on his trip to the Southwest, riding fast by another route, so as to pass Operator 5's caravan. He stopped in the places along Jimmy's proposed itinerary, and contacted politicians whom he knew, arranging for them to foment the discontent and trouble which Operator 5 later encountered when he arrived.

In the meantime, Hank Sheridan kept working hard, fighting against sabotage and internal dissension, to make his country strong again. The first consignments of refined gasoline had come in to New York from the Pennsylvania oil fields, and Hank stored these carefully, for future use. There would be plenty of demand for them. New shops were opened, and many dismantled airplanes put together and repaired. These planes would soon be able to take to the air, using the gasoline, and drop supplies to localities virtually cut off from the rest of the country. Tractors could be put into use on farms once more, and a

OPERATOR 5

hundred other advances could be made once the flow of gasoline became regular.

The news from Europe was good. England was rebuilding her empire, and France had reverted to republican form of government. True, countries like Italy and Germany, with some of the Balkan states, were once more choosing the dictatorial form of government; but with England and France working together, Hank Sheridan did not fear encroachment at this time from any of the Fascist countries.

Also heartening was the news that Russia and China had broken away from the Purple Empire, and were striking out for themselves. Europe was in better condition than we were, due to the fact that their resources had not been destroyed in a prolonged war. Great Britain, having come into possession of many of the huge battleships of the Empire, was once more a naval power, and there was talk of her sending a convoy of merchant ships to our shores with goods that we might need in rebuilding the ruins of our country.

Hank was negotiating for this when, late in December, the beacon communication system between New York and Operator 5's caravan was suddenly broken. The breaks occurred at half a dozen places at once, as if inspired by a single mind. Then all word from the caravan ceased to come in. The last Hank had heard was that Jimmy was heading west from Tulsa, still a thousand miles from Santa Fe. The country there was dangerous and lawless, and Hank could not tell whether the caravan had survived or perished.

He was beside himself with anxiety, but there was no way to

REVOLT OF THE DEVIL MEN

get word through. Courier after courier had failed to return or be heard from; and men whom he sent out to investigate the breaks in the beacon system also disappeared as if swallowed up by a giant maw.

General Ferrara reported that unrest was becoming rife in the city once more, and he counseled declaring martial law. But Hank Sheridan would not have it.

"This is a democratic form of government," he told Ferrara, "and we're going to keep it that way as long as we're in office!"

Ferrara spread his hands helplessly. "But we've got to protect the city against an uprising. Mark my words, sir, there's disaster coming!"

FERRARA'S WORDS of prophecy proved themselves true very shortly. It was the day before Christmas that Blaintree and his Brown Shirts struck. The city was in more or less festive mood. For the first time in three years, people had an opportunity to celebrate Christmas in fitting fashion, and under the American flag. Sheridan ordered extra rations distributed, and a great Christmas tree was put up in front of the Post Office Building. Men knocked off work early, and took their families for a walk along the newly built streets, wearing some of the heavy winter clothes fabricated in the factories which Hank Sheridan had had the foresight to put in operation.

Only a skeleton force of armed men was kept on duty to patrol the streets, most of them being given a furlough until the next evening.

And this was the time for which Blaintree had been waiting!

By two's and three's, his Brown Shirts filtered into the city, carrying arms concealed under their overcoats. They waited until seven o'clock, when families were at home over their Christmas dinners. Then Major Corvallo, with a picked group of hard-bitten rascals, invaded the Post Office Building. They stormed the building, firing as they came, and that was the signal for the Brown Shirts, distributed about the city to attack, seizing the key posts.

Corvallo led his gang into Sheridan's office, shooting down the few guards in the building.

Hank Sheridan didn't have a chance. He rose from the seat at his desk when Corvallo burst in. He saw the look in the major's face, and knew there was no hope for him. He sighed deeply, and said, "Well, I've tried hard. I'll leave it for Operator 5 to avenge me!"

Corvallo grinned like a wolf, and shot him down....

At the same time that this was taking place, other groups of Brown Shirts were raiding the storehouses, the arsenal, and the docks where the newly built ships were tied up. A special detail captured tanks where Hank Sheridan had stored the gasoline sent in from Pennsylvania.

In two hours the city was theirs, though sporadic fighting continued for several days, wherever loyal men held out. The populace of the city soon perceived that the Brown Shirts were not going to change the conditions against which they had been protesting. In fact, conditions became much worse.

Martial law was at once declared, and Blaintree was named President by a caucus of the Brown Shirt Party.

The new President immediately proceeded to issue a series

of edicts, conscripting all able-bodied men for labor battalions and military service. Hundreds of men who remained loyal to the democratic form of government were executed, and a reign of terror was inaugurated.

Carefully planned uprisings in Philadelphia, Baltimore, Hartford, Albany and Boston were staged at the same time, and the whole of the eastern seaboard, as far south as Norfolk, came into the hands of the new dictatorship. It was a dictatorship of iron and blood. Arrests took place in wholesale fashion, and men were shot for the slightest criticism of the government.

The Brown Shirts brought their three tanks out of hiding, and put them in shape; they drilled their military conscripts ruthlessly, in a frenzied effort to whip an army into shape. Men wondered to what purpose this army was to be put. And they soon had their answer. Late in January, three divisions, totaling thirty thousand men, under the command of Major Corvallo—now General Corvallo—set out toward the Southwest.

Corvallo was marching to attack Operator 5!

Blaintree accompanied the army. Operator 5 was the one factor that Blaintree feared. For Jimmy Christopher was immensely popular with the people, and, if he were left free to do as he willed, there was the chance that he could recruit enough men to wipe out the new dictatorship. It was to forestall this that the Brown Shirt divisions were marching. Blaintree and Corvallo planned to take Operator 5 by surprise. They had seen to it that all communication with the caravan was cut off. Dr. Oliver had done his work well. The beacon system was wrecked; no couriers were allowed through. The Brown Shirts hoped to reach the Southwest by forced marches, before Operator 5 even knew that there had been revolution at home—and to wipe him out!

They had seized all available auto trucks, using the precious supply of gasoline to mechanize their three divisions, taking it away from the constructive work for which Hank Sheridan had earmarked it. In addition, their three tanks would be of inestimable service in winning a decisive victory. Corvallo planned to fight the rest of the country into submission, and had a very good chance of doing it—for in all the land there were not three divisions of mechanized infantry in a single unit.

So it was that the new year saw a great engine of destruction rolling across the country to overtake Operator 5 and his caravan of mercy….

CHAPTER 7
THE THREAT FROM THE SKY

A LONG line of horsemen, rifles under their arms, was splashed by the multitudinous colors of the rising sun. Crossing a ridge, their leader threw up an arm in signal to halt, and the column closed in, but did not dismount. Behind the horsemen, as far as the eye could see into the brilliance of the sun's radiance, the rutted road was filled with slow-moving, heavily laden wagons whose canvas covering was bleached by exposure to a hundred suns, torn and shredded by a thousand winds. The men in the caravan were weary, gaunt, and parched. The teams of horses pushed into the rising heat with a stolid effort that belied the ten months of constant traveling which had gone before. Had an observer possessed the power to look backward upon the Santa Fe Trail, back through Tulsa, and through the Ozarks, across the Mississippi and beyond toward the east, he would have been amazed and startled to see the hospital units, food warehouses, industrious farms, orderly civilization which this column was creating as it marched. For where the caravan had passed, civilization once more dared to raise its head, and men ceased to live like beasts.

For three months now the column had been cut off from New York. No word had come through, either by courier or by beacon signal. Between here and the Mississippi, communications were still intact. But east of the Father of Waters, there was no longer a chain of beacons.

Operator 5 had no means of knowing whether the seeds that he had planted east of the Mississippi were bearing fruit, or whether they were withering under the frost of civil war. He knew very well that something was radically wrong in New York—otherwise, President Sheridan would have found some means to resume communications. And as he moved westward, he found, each day, that his beacon signal chain was becoming shorter and shorter.

But he was only one man, and he could not perform the impossible. He had brought relief and sanitation, and a chance to use the expert knowledge of technicians, to many hundreds of communities along the route of the caravan. He could not stay and make sure that proper use was made of those things which he had brought. He must move on, for farther westward other lands were crying for relief.

And now, while his column halted behind him, he stared far ahead at the plain which unfolded before him from the foot of the ridge where the Canadian River turned obliquely northward, cutting off the mesas to the east from the rest of New Mexico.

Pinyon and cedar trees spread here abundantly, their topmost branches flecked with the bold colorings of the rising sun. Beyond the plains, were the dim lights of the old city of Santa Fe, still cloaked in darkness under the great shadow of the lordly Sangre de Cristo Mountains, which towered into the night, as if brooding over the secrets locked in the breast of the badlands.

ANDY BRETTON, one-eyed Frank Simms and Tobias Follings crowded around Operator 5 as he stared out into the dissolving darkness ahead of them. Jimmy Christopher raised a hand, and pointed toward Santa Fe.

"There's our goal, boys," he said wearily. "We've done it. We've started America on the road back to civilization. We've practically built towns, and laid the foundations for hospitals and laboratories and schools. We've shown them how to reopen flooded mines, and how to drill for oil. We've started a stream of oil and coal flowing eastward that will provide power for factories and ships. We've saved thousands of men and women and children from starvation and freezing. Whatever else happens, boys, they can't take away from us what we've done!"

The other nodded in grave assent. All felt, as did Jimmy Christopher, that they were making history—history of a sort that is not often given credit in the text books, but which has made the wheels of the world go round since the beginning of time.

Only Tobias Follings had an ironic note to strike. "All this that we're doing, Operator 5—do you realize how easy it would be to wipe it out?"

"What do you mean?"

Follings smiled thinly. "What do you think is happening in New York? We've been away almost a year. They've had plenty of time to make progress, to develop. But suppose a man like Blaintree gets control there? He'll have the advantage of all raw materials we've been pouring back east! He'll have the modern machinery of peace and also of—*war!*"

Frank Simms and Andy Bretton laughed, nervously.

"Bosh! Hank is too well liked. No one could get control away from him!" said Andy.

But Jimmy Christopher shook his head. "Don't you remember Doctor Oliver, back there at Union City? He was traveling ahead of us. We never did catch up with him. Didn't you notice how there were always some trouble-makers wherever we stopped? Oliver was the one who put Cutler up to waylaying us, Andy. Oliver didn't do that just for a whim. He was working with a deep purpose. I don't forget that Oliver was one of Blaintree's chief supporters when he was trying to get the Continental Congress to elect him President. I know that there was a plot on foot in New York when we left. I sent Diane and Tim to look into it, and they never got back."

Jimmy sighed. "It's entirely possible that there's a new regime in New York now. And—" he paused a moment to let the next

OPERATOR 5

words sink in—"it's also entirely possible that all of us will find there is a price on our heads when we return east!"

The column behind was spreading out, the wagons moving out to form a circle, as they did whenever they camped. The men and horses had traveled all through the night, and were weary and hungry.

"This is as good a place to stop for breakfast as any," Jimmy told the others. "There's still a good twenty miles to Santa Fe."

He focused his glasses on the trail over the plains, and spotted a small group of horsemen riding toward them. "That'll be George Macklin coming back with some of the officials from the city."

Just then Lieutenant Larry Bridges came running up, his face flushed with excitement. "Operator 5!" he exclaimed. "I just set up my heliograph set, and I got in touch with Amarillo. Our man there says four airplanes have just passed over the town, heading in this direction!"

Jimmy Christopher's eyes narrowed. "Planes! There hasn't been a plane in the air for two years!"

Both the American Defense Force and the invading armies had ceased to use planes for combat almost a year before the end of the war.

With the dwindling and then the gradual disappearance of oil reserves, the supply of gasoline for planes had been cut off. Planes had lain in open fields, rotting and deteriorating, so that even after the first supplies of oil became available again, as a result of Jimmy Christopher's development of the Pennsylvania fields, there had not been a plane in the east capable of taking to the air.

And now, abruptly, four of them were thundering westward toward their column, without warning.

Operator 5 thought quickly. "It's two hundred miles to Amarillo," he said. Then, to Larry Bridges, "Did your man there say how long ago he sighted them?"

"Only ten minutes ago sir. They were flying high, and seemed to be coming from the direction of Tulsa."

Jimmy Christopher nodded thoughtfully, "That gives us about fifty minutes to prepare for them."

Andy Bretton asked tensely, "You think they mean us harm, sir? You think they might attack?"

Jimmy smiled, and glanced at Tobias Follings. "Remember what Follings just said? If someone in the east has planes, it means that they've made great strides forward in the year that we've been away. Now, logically thinking—if they've made such progress, they should have found a way to communicate with us before this. I'm sure that if Hank Sheridan were in command in New York, he'd have sent one of those planes ahead to bring us word of what was happening. And the fact that those planes didn't stop at Amarillo—didn't even drop a note—speaks for itself. Whoever is flying them is no friend of ours!"

Andy Bretton was excited. "Then what'll we do?"

"We'll not give them a chance to bomb us!" Jimmy said grimly. He issued curt orders to Captain Bretton. "Send back word not to encamp, Andy. Tell the boys not to stake out the

OPERATOR 5

kitchens, but to hand out dry rations. I want everybody ready to move in twenty minutes!"

Andy Bretton saluted, and swung his mount toward the rear.

Jimmy Christopher went on with his orders. "Simms, you get hold of all the marksmen in the column who have high-powered rifles. Have them take up positions in the shelter of trees or rocks, and be prepared to pepper those planes if they try to *strafe* us. And you, Follings, get a detail of men out to cut down underbrush. We're going to spread the wagons, and camouflage them so they won't attract attention from the air!"

The men saluted, and hurried to obey the orders. They knew as well as he did, that those planes might and might not be unfriendly. Operator 5 was going to a lot of trouble to guard against a danger which might not materialize. But that thoroughness of his had saved them from disaster many times on the long trek into the southwest.

NOW JIMMY CHRISTOPHER spoke to Larry Bridges. "You, Larry, get back to the heliograph, and resume communication with Amarillo. Try to get any information you can that will give us a clue to the identity of those planes. Ask them to try to flash back to Tulsa, and to other towns to the east, and to find out if any troop movements have been observed recently."

"Troop movements?" Bridges asked, puzzled.

Jimmy nodded. "Those planes didn't fly out of nowhere, Larry. They've got a base somewhere. What I'm afraid of is that they may be scouts for some body of troops that's marching in our direction."

"But why—"

REVOLT OF THE DEVIL MEN

"I'll tell you why," Operator 5 said grimly. "Suppose you were Frederick Blaintree, and you had staged a revolt, and had seized power in New York. What would you do first?"

Bridges thought a moment, his forehead wrinkled. "I guess I'd try to consolidate my position—eliminate all opposition—"

"That's it!" Jimmy Christopher cut in sharply. "And Blaintree or anyone else who might overthrow Hank Sheridan and declare himself dictator—would know that I'd never let it ride—that I'd move heaven and earth to restore democracy, and to avenge Hank. So the first think he'd try to do would be to eliminate this caravan.

"He'd also try to extend his sway over the Southwest, which is virgin territory, and which can furnish him with the greatest amount of raw material, if properly developed. Therefore, the first thing he'd do would be to organize an expedition to destroy us."

"I get it!" Bridges said.

"It's all supposition," Jimmy went, "but we can't afford to overlook any bets. So you get on that heliograph, and try to pick up all the information you can."

Bridges started to leave, and Jimmy called him back. "Another thing, Larry. When you go by, tell Andy to leave three or four wagons out here on the ridge—without camouflage. We'll keep them there as a sort of test. If the planes are friendly—all right. If they're enemies, they'll try to attack the wagons, and we'll know where we stand."

Lieutenant Bridges grinned, appreciating the strategy. "Right, sir!" He saluted, and hurried his horse back toward the column.

OPERATOR 5

Jimmy Christopher was left alone for a moment. Now that the others could not see him, he allowed the mask of inscrutability, with which he had shrouded himself, to drop from his face. Utter weariness showed in his features.

His shoulders drooped. He had had enough of all this strife. For two years he had fought like a Trojan to defend the country against a ruthless foreign enemy. And then, for another year he had worked ceaselessly to rebuild the country, laboring under the handicap of lack of materials and lack of power. Then, for the past ten months he had led this long caravan on its arduous, thankless task, through two thousand miles of desolated territory. He was tired of it all. But he never dared to let any of his lieutenants see how he felt. To them he was the spirit of buoyancy, good cheer, hope and electric vitality. It was he who raised their spirits when they were dejected; he who instilled them with new enthusiasm when they were almost licked by some seemingly insurmountable obstacle.

But superb actor that he was, he felt that he would not be able to keep playing his part much longer. For one thing, ever since he had given up hope of seeing Diane or Tim alive again, something had gone out of his life. He did not feel that vivid enthusiasm for his work that he had felt in the old days. He realized now, more strongly than ever before, how much he needed the love, confidence and courageous smile of Diane Elliot.

He sighed and squared his shoulders. The delegation from Santa Fe was approaching, with George Macklin riding in the lead, and he must not show them how he felt.

By the time they reached him, there was nothing of the

dejected attitude left in his appearance. They saw only a trim, efficient man whose reputation had gone before him, and whose quiet, cool, appraising eyes measured them accurately.

GEORGE MACKLIN performed the introductions, "This is Mayor Delcourt, the mayor of Santa Fe," Macklin said, indicating a big, heavy man who sat his horse as if his weight of almost two hundred pounds meant nothing.

Mayor Delcourt reached over his pommel and gripped Jimmy's hand firmly. "Welcome to Santa Fe, Operator 5. We've heard stories of the troubles you've encountered in the other towns along your route. I want to tell you—" Delcourt's voice boomed out with the sincerity and the resonance of truth—"that you won't find any such trouble in Santa Fe. We're starving—I'll tell you that. And we are thankful that you and your boys had the stamina and the courage to cover two thousand miles to reach us with food." Delcourt smiled under his flowing mustache. "You'll get plenty of cooperation from us out here, Operator 5!"

Jimmy Christopher returned that smile warmly. "Those words are music to my ears!" he said. He led Delcourt and the delegation back toward the wagon which he used as an office on the trek, and they squatted under the torn canvas top, while a cook's assistant brought them hot coffee. There was no sugar or cream with the coffee, but Delcourt smacked his lips.

"Operator 5, it's two years since I've tasted a cup of Java! Did you bring a lot of it?"

"We have a good supply," Jimmy assured him. "But now, I've got something more serious to talk to you about."

OPERATOR 5

Delcourt caught the serious tone of his voice. He finished his coffee, put down the cup. "Shoot!" he said tersely.

Jimmy spoke swiftly, telling him what he suspected the situation in New York to be, telling him of the sabotage of Doctor Oliver along the route of the caravan, and finally telling him of the planes that were approaching.

"You can see by looking out the rear of this wagon," he finished, "that the caravan is being broken up and camouflaged. But that is only a minor matter. If it should turn out that those planes are the advance guard of a military force, we'll have to fight. I have only a hundred riflemen. Can you raise any fighting men down here, Delcourt?"

The mayor of Santa Fe sat silent for an instant. His eyes studied those of Jimmy Christopher. Then he spoke slowly. "If what you suspect turns out to be so, Operator 5, I can promise you the support of every man with a gun in the Southwest! We've had to fight for a living down here, for two years. We've had to fight nature, and we've had to fight the disbanded raiding guerrillas of the Purple armies. We've fought hard, and we've endured much—but through it all we kept our liberty."

Delcourt's face flushed. "We've kept our liberty, and—" his voice rose slightly—"by God, we'll fight to keep it against any slimy rats who come in here and try to establish a dictatorship! I can speak for every man in the Southwest. We're with you, Operator 5!"

Jimmy Christopher smiled. "I knew that would be your answer!"

Instinctively, the two men shook hands again, their eyes

meeting. It was a silent pledge of mutual loyalty, by two men who loved their country well enough to risk everything for her.

CHAPTER 8
THE HAWKS FLY WITH DEATH!

IT SEEMED almost as if none of the other men in that delegation existed or mattered. There were three of them, and they approved of Delcourt's position, for each nodded in approval of that handclasp. But it was apparent that they followed Delcourt's leadership blindly, just as Andy Bretton and the others did with Operator 5.

It was Hugh Delcourt in whom they had confidence, and his solid, uncompromising appearance indicated that their confidence was not misplaced. Jimmy Christopher had judged Delcourt quickly and accurately, as a man to be depended upon. Here, in the midst of desolation, two men met and shook hands, and unbeknownst to them—that handclasp settled the faith of a nation.

Now the faint drone of airplane motors came to their ears, and they listened tautly for an instant. Then Operator 5 sprang into action.

They leaped from the wagon, and Jimmy cast a quick glance about.

His orders had been carried out with smooth efficiency. Most of the wagons had been driven off the ridge, and he could see where they had been staked out here and there along the road, near clumps of cedars whose branches shielded them from observation by the air.

All was in order.

Bretton and Simms and Follings had done their work well. Though it was easy to spot the wagons from here, it would be very difficult—almost impossible—to do so from the air, unless the planes knew they were in the neighborhood and flew very low.

Four of the wagons, including the one which served as Jimmy's office, had been left on the ridge, and the teams of horses had been unhitched. Here and there, Jimmy could see where Andy Bretton had placed his marksmen. They were sitting or lying, immovable, rifles at cheeks, peering up into the sky at the three giant shapes whose shadows were spewed upon the earth by the crimson sun.

Jimmy Christopher's eyes narrowed as he gazed up at the ships. They were three Boeing pursuit planes, of the type used in the early days of the war, rebuilt and reconditioned—and Jimmy knew at once that they had not been outfitted by Hank Sheridan. For he and Hank had often discussed the time when they would turn to the task of equipping an air fleet for America, and both agreed that the most logical thing to do would be to assemble the parts of the Fallada tri-motored pursuits and bombers of the Purple Empire, of which there were complete stores of parts in a warehouse in Hoboken, abandoned by the departed enemy.

Those Falladas were the ultimate in flying craft, and far superior to these antiquated Boeings. Besides, the parts were new and unused, and could easily have been assembled once a going factory plant was available. The presence of those Fallada parts was not generally known, and anyone else outfitting a group of planes would naturally choose the Boeings, which were next best. But that very fact convinced Operator 5 that these ships had not been commissioned by President Sheridan.

He spoke of this quickly to Hugh Delcourt, as they stood there and watched them, and Delcourt's eyes smoldered. "That means that we have to fight!" he said grimly.

"We'll soon see!" Jimmy Christopher told him. He motioned to Frank Simms, who had come running up toward them, with a dozen men.

"Set up the machine guns, Frank. We're going to have to use them for the first time!"

They had taken along three machine guns, with part of the small store of ammunition still available for them. Up to now they had not had to break them out. But though they had not yet had occasion to use them, Jimmy Christopher, with his usual thoroughness, had held frequent machine-gun drill, until all the men of the column had become expert in setting them up for combat.

Now, under Frank Simms' crisp orders, the guns came out of one of the wagons, and were up in three separated spots on the ridge, within three minutes.

THE PLANES overhead were circling high, apparently having spotted the four wagons on the ridge. Now one of them came down in a power dive. Operator 5 and Hugh Delcourt

OPERATOR 5

The tank loomed above them—he couldn't free her!

remained standing where they were, staring up, in utter disregard of the danger of that diving plane.

The ship came down to five hundred feet and leveled off, and they could see the pilot's helmeted head peering over the side, as well as that of his observer. They saw the machine guns mounted forward. The pilot raised a hand in signal to the other two planes.

Then all at once, the three planes were coming down in a

OPERATOR 5

whining power dive, pointing their noses directly at the wagons! Their machine guns began to spit long before they could possibly be effective. Jimmy Christopher cast a quick glance at Delcourt, and smiled grimly.

"They're novices!" he shouted above the roar of the diving motors. He shook his head in the negative toward Frank Simms, who was commanding the machine guns. "Don't shoot yet!" he yelled.

Now the planes were closer to the ground, and their leaden hail began to spatter everywhere. Jimmy Christopher dragged Delcourt to the ground, motioned the others in the delegation to drop, too.

Then, when the planes were low enough so that it was possible to see the details of the landing gear, Jimmy Christopher raised a hand in signal to his machine gunners.

From three sides of a well-planned triangle, the machine-gun bullets drummed upward into the air in a death-dealing flurry, the chattering of the ground guns joining the staccato bark of those in the planes, and mingling with the roaring drone of the motors.

The ships were diving in line, and Jimmy's gunners kept their stream of lead concentrated at one place, almost directly above his wagon. Each of those planes had to pass through that field of fire in order to come out of its dive, and each one received its baptism of deadly lead.

In a second the power dives were over, the ships were zooming upward. Two of them had received death-blows. Black smoke billowed from their tails. One did not succeed in coming out of the dive at all, but crashed into a cedar tree at the edge of the ridge, bursting into flames. The other rose almost to a thousand feet, and then seemed to fall apart in the air.

The third got away safely, and hovered high above, circling a moment as if in indecision. Then it turned abruptly, and winged toward the east whence it had come.

Jimmy Christopher and the others leaped to their feet. Frank Simms and his machine gunners came running, doing a jig in their exultant excitement. All ran to the burning plane. It was a mass of crisp cinders now, but the body of the observer had fallen some fifty feet from the ship. He was dead, but the Brown Shirt uniform on him was distinctly visible, its hawk-insignia on the armband.

Jimmy Christopher said, "That's what I expected. The Brown Shirt revolution!"

Hugh Delcourt gripped his arm. "Operator 5, this is all I wanted to know. I'm going back to Santa Fe and start recruiting. There are thousands of men in from the backwoods and from the desert, waiting for your caravan. Every one of those men will be ready and willing to fight. Do you want them?"

Jimmy laughed. "Do I want them! We'll give the Brown Shirts a real surprise!"

DELCOURT LEFT for Santa Fe with his delegation, and Jimmy Christopher went into conference with his lieutenants. It was a few minutes later that Larry Bridges came up to him with a slip of paper. His face was pale. "I've been in touch with Amarillo again, sir. They—they've got bad news. Here's the message they sent through."

OPERATOR 5

Jimmy took the message, and read it aloud to the others—

BROWN SHIRT ARMY OF THIRTY THOUSAND UNDER GENERAL CORVALLO NOW AT TULSA. FREDERICK BLAINTREE WITH ARMY. ANNOUNCES HE HAS BEEN CHOSEN PRESIDENT BY BROWN SHIRT PARTY IN PLACE OF PRESIDENT SHERIDAN WHO IS DEAD. THEY HAVE FORMED CORPORATIVE STATE WITH BLAINTREE AT HEAD. THEY ARE CONSCRIPTING MEN FOR MILITARY SERVICE AND FOR LABOR THEY HAVE CONFISCATED ALL SUPPLIES LEFT BY YOUR CARAVAN ON THE LINE OF MARCH. CORVALLO BOASTS HE WILL WIPE YOU OUT WITHIN ONE WEEK...
TRUMAN, AMARILLO.

When Operator 5 stopped reading, there was silence in the little group of lieutenants. Then Follings breathed, "Thirty thousand men! My God, what can we do against an army like that?"

But Jimmy Christopher was not thinking of this. He was thinking of the line in the message which announced that President Sheridan was dead. Suddenly there was a great empty void in his heart. He and Hank had stood together for a long time. He had seen Hank Sheridan rise from the position of small-town mayor to that of President of the United States. He had seen how steadfast and loyal a friend Hank could be. That he should have met death at the hands of these rats of Brown Shirts made him see red!

The others watched silently. They saw the great sorrow in

his eyes, and sympathized with him. At last, Andy Bretton said gently, "We'll avenge Hank Sheridan all right. Hank would fight—even against odds of thirty thousand. We'll do the same."

Jimmy Christopher paced up and down. "Fight? Yes. We'll fight those Brown Shirts right here. It'll be a hopeless fight, and it's probably the end for all of us." He paused and faced the others. "But I know you boys pretty well. I don't think any of you cares to live under a dictator!"

Tobias Follings switched the cud of chewing tobacco in his mouth, and spat. "Hell, no! Might's well be dead, as that way. We'll fight!"

The others chorused Follings' agreement.

Jimmy Christopher nodded. "Send a messenger to Delcourt. Tell him the situation. Let him explain it to his men. And if they want to join us, fine. If not, we'll fight alone!"

He swung to face Andy Bretton. "Now, Andy, what do you say if you and I take a little ride?"

Andy's eyes opened wide. "Ride? You mean—" his face broke into a grin—"we're going scouting?"

Jimmy nodded. "Just the two of us. I want to take a look at this army of Corvallo's. All we have to go by is this report from Amarillo. I like to see what I'm going to have to fight!"

Andy Bretton turned swiftly and directed an orderly to bring up two fresh horses, saddled and fully equipped.

"I'm leaving you in command, Follings," Operator 5 said.

Tobias Follings scowled sourly. "I'm not hankering for the job, Operator 5. Why can't you send someone else instead of going yourself? I don't like the responsibility—"

OPERATOR 5

"You'll take it and like it!" Jimmy told him, smiling. He slapped the other's back affectionately. "You're a damned good soldier, Tobias. I've seen you handle a regiment of your Pennsylvania infantry, and I know."

The fresh horses were brought up, and Operator 5 rode off with Andy Bretton at his side.

Tobias Follings stood there looking after them for a long while, until they faded from view. Then he shook his head somberly. "I don't like it," he muttered. "I have a feeling in my bones that those two are riding into… hell!"

CHAPTER 9
THE JAWS OF HELL

OPERATOR 5 had more than one reason for going on that scouting expedition with Andy Bretton. True, he felt it imperative to gain advance information of the strength and make-up of Corvallo's force, at first hand, rather than rely solely upon the report from Amarillo. But there was also another motive. In spite of his apparent confidence, he had little hope of being able to defeat an army of thirty thousand with the few men at his disposal, or even with the additional force which Delcourt could bring to his support. There was also the thought in the back of his mind that perhaps he could find some weak spot in Corvallo's array.

So, when they glimpsed the first of the enemy scouting patrols, he and Andy Bretton took cover and allowed them to pass.

REVOLT OF THE DEVIL MEN

It was almost an hour after that they sighted the main force of Brown Guards. They were just breaking camp to resume the march, and Operator 5 with Andy pushed his horse up to the ridge of an overhanging rock in order to get a better view.

They could see the American flag near the headquarters tent. Beside the Stars and Stripes, however, there was another flag—the sight of which caused Jimmy Christopher to frown. It was a banner with a brown background, and emblazoned upon the field of brown was the figure of a black hawk.

Jimmy swept the enemy encampment with his glass, watching the buzzing activity keenly. Andy Bretton pulled his mount up close on the sloping rock, and said, "Corvallo has a powerful force there, Operator 5. Look at that infantry—they're all mechanized!"

Jimmy nodded grimly. "He's made use of the gasoline that we've been sending to New York. He's put all those trucks into operation with it—instead of keeping it for factory use, as Hank intended!"

They watched while regiment after regiment, spread out over the vast plain, moving out into marching order. Soon the road below was filled with vehicles. Because the road was torn up, their progress was necessarily slow; but it conserved the energy of the troops. They would be fresh when they arrived at the field of battle.

Andy Bretton pointed to a spot about a half mile behind the headquarters tent, where was visible an airplane. "It's probably the ship that escaped after attacking us," he said. "Looks like it's out of commission." He kept his glasses focused on it. "There's a bunch of mechanics working over it. Operator 5—they're dismantling and crating it! It must have been hit by our machine guns, and they can't repair it!"

Jimmy nodded. "That's a bit of a break. But if you'll look over to the west, you'll see some real grief for us!"

Bretton followed Jimmy's pointing finger, and cursed aloud. "Two whole batteries of six-inch guns! We'll have to stand a barrage."

"It's not the artillery, Andy," Operator 5 said tightly. "We could dig in and last out the barrage of six-inch guns."

"What then—"

"Just raise your glasses. Focus them on the road beyond those batteries. What do you see?"

Andy Bretton did as directed, and suddenly his hand shook. "Tanks!" he gasped. "Three tanks!"

"That's right, Andy—three baby tanks. Do you realize what they can do to us with those three tanks? They can drive right through our lines. Barbed wire won't hold them back, and the rifles of our boys won't stop them."

Andy Bretton lowered his glasses. "You're right, Operator 5." He was good enough soldier to realize that those three baby tanks could spell the difference between victory and defeat—if they came as a surprise. "We'll have to change our whole plan of defense—dig trenches instead of relying on barbed wire. We'll have to build high embankments to stop them—"

"Right! And we've got to get back to Santa Fe as fast as possible, and go to work. We won't have much time!"

Andy Bretton nodded. "Do we start now?"

REVOLT OF THE DEVIL MEN

His last word was drowned by the *spang* of a rifle bullet against the rock at his horse's feet. A second and third shot followed in quick succession.

OPERATOR 5 cast a quick glance to the east, and saw that a patrol of the enemy had sighted them and was galloping up, firing. It was only that which had saved their lives—otherwise the enemy marksmanship would have been better.

"Down to the road, quick!" Jimmy Christopher shouted. "We can just make it!"

Andy Bretton spurred his horse, and the mount, startled, shuffled and slipped. It went scuffling down the face of the rock, unable to stop on the smooth surface. Andy was thrown over its head, described a somersault in the air, and landed, dazed, upon his knees in the road below, less than fifty feet from the charging patrol.

The Brown Shirts raised a shout of triumph, and spurred their horses faster. Andy Bretton got to his feet groggy. His mount, a well-trained stallion, remained standing at his side until he touched the bridle. Almost automatically, Captain Bretton leaped into the saddle.

The patrol was almost upon him now. Their bayoneted guns were reaching for him. In an instant, they would have spitted him.

It was then that Operator 5 acted. His rifle was up, pumping shot after shot into the thickly massed patrol. Two, three, of the leaders went down under his fire, and for a moment were thrown back upon themselves, confused. It was still too late for Jimmy

OPERATOR 5

Christopher to get down off the rock and clear into the road, for the patrol was between himself and Bretton.

He shouted hoarsely, "Ride, Andy! Ride!"

Bretton started to shout an objection, but Operator 5's driving voice jarred him into silence. "Ride! One of us has to warn the caravan of the tanks!"

Andy Bretton understood. In order to save the caravan from the menace of the tanks, he must desert Operator 5!

Captain Bretton did the only thing left him to do. He whipped his horse, and sent it racing down the road. The patrol was straightened out now, and half of them went spurring after Andy, the others turning their fire upon Operator 5.

Jimmy had dismounted from his horse. He lay at full length on the rock, pumping shots, not at the detail that was storming his own position on the rock, but at those pursuing Andy Bretton. He must sell his own life dearly in order that Bretton should reach the caravan.

Coolly, deliberately, he fired his long-barreled Winchester, bringing down a man each time he pressed the trigger. He brought down every one of the six men spurring after Bretton. Now the way was clear for the young captain to return to the caravan.

But in performing that feat of cool marksmanship, Jimmy Christopher had deliberately sacrificed himself. The other half of the patrol was at the top of the rock and hurled themselves upon him before he could get to his feet.

Lying there on his face, with nothing left in his rifle, he had no chance. He had expected to be shot out of hand, by the first man to reach the top. Instead, he felt a cold gun muzzle at the back of his neck. A knee bored into his spine.

"You are the prisoner of the Brown Guard Army!"

OPERATOR 5'S Brown Shirt captors were in an ugly mood. They had just seen half their patrol decimated before their eyes by this man who faced them now without the flicker of an eyelash.

The leader of the detail, a short, burly corporal, stared at him savagely. "We ought to shoot your heart out. But General Corvallo issued orders to take some prisoners for questioning. That's the only reason you're alive!"

Jimmy Christopher smiled, but said nothing. He was hustled to his horse, mounted between two of the cavalrymen. They left their dead lying in the road, to be buried by the labor battalion which followed the army. They rode along the edge of the road, now clustered with troops, toward the rear of the line, where Corvallo and his staff were still encamped.

The patrol did not recognize him as Operator 5, but General Corvallo did the moment he was brought in. The Brown Shirt commander's eyes narrowed and he began to rub his hands in delight.

"Well, well," he said to the corporal. "You've done a good piece of work here!"

The corporal growled, "He killed eight of our men, General—"

"No matter, no matter!" Corvallo interrupted impatiently. "It would have been cheap at the price of fifty men. *This is Operator 5!*"

The corporal gasped, and grew pale. "Operator 5—himself!"

OPERATOR 5

"Himself!" Corvallo assured him, still smiling. "You are promoted as of this date to the rank of sergeant! Now—dismissed!"

The corporal backed out, dazed.

Corvallo motioned toward a camp chair, with exaggerated politeness. "Sit down, Operator 5. This is the best thing that has happened since the Brown Guard took over the government!"

Jimmy Christopher remained standing.

Corvallo seemed to be waiting for something. "I've sent for another friend of yours, who will be very pleased to see you here."

They remained thus, staring at each other, for several minutes, neither lowering his eyes. Corvallo, though he had a sentry at the door to protect him, began to fidget. At last he weakened—let his lids drop over his eyes. Then his face grew livid, as he took a step forward. He gripped the butt of the revolver in the holster at his side, and Jimmy laughed again. "Going to murder me—the way you murdered Hank Sheridan?"

Corvallo bared his teeth. The revolver was halfway out. Whether he would have shot or not, it is hard to say. He was stopped by the entrance of Frederick Blaintree.

BLAINTREE ALSO wore the uniform of a general of the Brown Guard. In addition, a short black cape fell from the shoulders down to his waist line. Embroidered upon the front of the cape was the black hawk emblem, with the words underneath, in Latin script: *Veni, vidi, vici.*

Jimmy Christopher smiled tauntingly at the new dictator of America.

"Another Caesar!" he remarked. "So you think you have the

right to use the words that Caesar used when he conquered Gaul!" Jimmy's lips twisted in scorn. "Why, you cheap, murderous politician! In Caesar's day, you would have been thrown to the lions!"

Blaintree's thin, cruel lips tightened. "I know you're a hard man to break, Operator 5. But, by God, I know how to do it!" He took a step closer. His voice came insidiously now. "You haven't heard anything from your sweetheart, Diane Elliot, or that brat, Tim Donovan—have you?"

Jimmy Christopher's heart skipped a beat, but he kept his poker face. Even his eyes did not betray the sudden tumult in his breast. His voice was level when he spoke. "I'm sure *you* can't tell me anything about them that I don't know."

Blaintree smirked, and winked at Corvallo. "No? Then, listen. You sent them both up to Yonkers to spy on me. They watched a review of Brown Guard troops in the Empire City race track, and then they tried to escape. They were captured by my men, Operator 5, in the old Kensico aqueduct. Tim was wounded, and they couldn't escape. They were easily caught." He leaned even closer. "What do you think I did with them?"

Jimmy Christopher's blood was racing. His hands were flat open at his sides, and he refrained from clenching them only with a great effort. He did not want the dictator to see his emotion. "If you've harmed them, Blaintree, I give you my solemn word that I'll throttle you to death with my own hands!"

Blaintree laughed. "You're in no position to make threats. What if I told you they were still alive?" His eyes gleamed.

OPERATOR 5

Jimmy didn't answer, but kept his eyes fixed on the other's, trying to bore into his mind and read the truth.

Blaintree went on gloatingly, "What if I told you they had been executed as spies?"

Still, Jimmy didn't answer.

Blaintree laughed, and winked once more at Corvallo. "I think we know how to break him down. We'll keep him incommunicado until tomorrow, when we come within striking distance of his caravan. Then we'll make him a proposition—eh?"

Corvallo rubbed his hands. "A damned good idea, Blaintree. Maybe we can make a deal with this last of the patriots!"

He summoned the corporal, and ordered him to take Jimmy Christopher to one of the ammunition trucks and keep him handcuffed inside it during the march to Santa Fe.

The last thing that Jimmy heard, as he was led out between the double file of guards, was the triumphant laughter of Dictator Blaintree and General Corvallo.

OUTSIDE HEADQUARTERS tent, columns of troops were moving past steadily in the growing darkness. Gun carriages clattered, trucks creaked and small arms clanked—but there was no singing. It was as if this army, recruited by a rapacious dictator, lived only in the bitterness and hatred fostered by its leaders.

His captors marched Jimmy diagonally across a field toward a side road where the ammunition trucks were moving. These were apparently being routed along another road so as not to be too near the main body of troops. They found a half-empty ammunition truck, and the corporal gruffly motioned Jimmy inside, followed him in, while the rest of the detail remained on the ground.

It was dark under the canvas cover, and Jimmy could discern the piles of six-inch shells in the front of the chassis. The rear was empty. The corporal had no handcuffs, but produced a length of hemp. He pushed Jimmy into the interior of the truck, until their feet were touching the pile of shells, indicating the stanchion at the side.

"Wrap your hands around that," he growled. "We'll keep you safe, all right. Boy, this is my big day! To capture Operator 5 and—"

He never finished.

Operator 5's bunched fist came up in the darkness like a driving piston, thudding against the side of his jaw. The corporal's head snapped back like a mechanical toy. It cracked against the very stanchion to which he had intended to bind his captive's hands. He collapsed, inert, upon the pile of shells.

Jimmy did not stop moving even while the corporal was falling. His racing hands ripped off his own tunic, and then he stooped, pulled over the unconscious man's body, and peeled off the brown shirt.

The men outside were not suspicious as yet, but Jimmy had to work fast. He slipped into the Brown Guard's tunic, strapped on the man's revolver, and jammed the corporal's cap on his own head. In the fast gathering darkness, with the cap over his eyes, he might just be able to pass for the corporal.

With his hand on the butt of his gun, Jimmy backed out of the truck. He could hear the voices of the rest of the detail

OPERATOR 5

behind him in the darkness. One called out, "Got him safe, Kriss?"

Jimmy only grunted an answer. He dropped to the ground, but, instead of moving to rejoin the others, walked swiftly around the end of the truck, moving up toward the driver's cab in front.

One of the men shouted, "Hey, Kriss—where you going? We're shovin' off already!"

Jimmy didn't reply. He was at the front now, and leaped up into the cab. He had his gun out, ready to smash at the driver if there should be one. But there was no one in the driver's seat. Evidently one of this detail was to have driven the truck.

Operator 5 smiled grimly. He turned the ignition switch, kicked over the motor. He cut in the headlights, illuminating the road, clear ahead of him. Above the roar of the motor, he heard the excited shouts of the soldiers, but paid them no attention. He was accelerating up to thirty, within fifty feet, roaring down the road toward the west.

For a hundred yards he traveled unmolested, and then a bullet whined past his cheek, smashed at the windshield, spreading a fine spider's web of cracks, but doing no other damage to the shatterproof glass. Other bullets followed, but Operator 5 hunched low over the wheel, eyes glued ahead.

There were perhaps fifteen trucks on the road ahead of him, but moving in a slow single line, leaving the left hand side clear for fast couriers of staff cars. It was this lane that Jimmy followed, and, before the drivers of the other trucks realized what had taken place, he was past them, with nothing before him but a possible patrol or two, and then—Santa Fe!

CHAPTER 10
LIBERTY'S LAST STAND

IT WAS thirty miles from Santa Fe that Operator 5 met Andy Bretton and his company of a hundred men riding east. Andy had recruited them to come back for the attempt to rescue him!

Operator 5 swallowed hard when he learned their intended mission. "Good old Andy!"

The return to the caravan was more in the nature of a triumphal procession. Follings and the others had given Jimmy Christopher up for lost, after hearing Andy Bretton's tale. Bretton had blamed himself for having left his chief to be captured—though all agreed it was the only course open. Without warning of the tanks, the caravan's defenses would have amounted to nothing more than a cardboard breastwork.

Now Follings gladly turned back the full responsibility of the defense to Jimmy Christopher. Scouts were thrown out, and reported that the main column of the enemy was bogged down in mud about seventy miles east—that it would take them at least two or three more days to reach Santa Fe. This was good news, for it offered a respite, and Jimmy could perfect the plans for resistance.

The next two days were feverish ones for Operator 5 and his men. Jimmy selected the spot where they had encamped as the best site for the forthcoming battle. Since the enemy was coming to him, he had the choice of the battle ground, and judged that this position would be as difficult for them to take as any other. Besides, it was at a good distance from Santa Fe and the women and children there would be out of danger.

There were three ridges here, each of which could be stubbornly defended. The approach to all three was open, and an attacking force would find little cover. He had originally sent men scouring all through the cattle country to rip out wire fences, which he used to lay down barbed-wire entanglements in the fields surrounding his positions. Now he supplemented the barbed-wire with a well planned system of trenches and breastworks, where riflemen could lie, and keep up a continuous fire, while at the same time, protected from the rolling tanks.

Hourly, the recruits kept pouring out from Santa Fe, and, as the news spread through the surrounding country, more and more mounted men kept turning up. Delcourt's promise had not been an empty one. In four days close to five thousand patriots reported for service. These were quiet, stubborn plainsmen, hunters, ex-soldiers of the American Defense Force—even a contingent of Mescalero Indians from the reservation near Carrizozo, far to the south. In all these men there still burned the fierce desire for liberty—a democratic government *sans* dictators, where a man could live at peace with his neighbor, yet enjoy personal freedom.

They knew the odds against them—that a formidable army was marching upon them, equipped with a certain amount of modern tools of warfare, which they, themselves did not possess.

REVOLT OF THE DEVIL MEN

They realized that five thousand men were all too few to stand against thirty thousand, with field artillery tanks. They fully understood that the ruthless policy of the dictator would mete out death to them in the event of defeat. Yet they chose to fight under Operator 5 rather than bow to an autocrat.

Operator 5, himself, entertained little hope of victory. But he planned carefully and well. In the event of defeat, he did not intend to leave the field of battle alive. In truth, he had little left for which to live. Since his conversation with Corvallo and Blaintree, he fully believed that Diane and Tim were dead by now; and with the news of the death of Hank Sheridan, desire for life had utterly left him.

Jimmy had everything in readiness by the fifth day. His machine guns were placed, riflemen in position, cavalry in reserve behind each of the ridges. The covered wagons were ready to be hooked with the long teams of horses, and loaded with riflemen. Those covered wagons were to play an important part in the battle. Since he did not have tanks, he was going to have chariots! That was his scheme!

When Delcourt and the others first heard his idea, they were eager to volunteer for service on the chariots. It was planned that, if there should be the opportunity, those covered wagons would come tearing out along lanes in the barbed-wire, to hurl themselves upon the enemy just as had been the custom of the chariots of the Greek warriors. Jimmy had no difficulty in selecting a thousand men to man the wagons.

Now his scouts began to bring in reports of the approaching enemy. There were clashes between their advance guard and the

OPERATOR 5

scouts, but Jimmy gave strict orders that his own men should always fall back. He didn't want to precipitate the battle and, for that reason, refrained from sending out strong detachments which might become embroiled with enemy divisions and make it necessary for him to abandon his carefully prepared position in hurrying to their rescue.

NOW, ON the fifth day, he stood upon Ridge Number One—the original ridge where he had first met Delcourt—and surveyed all of his arrangements, giving last-minute orders to his lieutenants. Andy Bretton was in command of Ridge Number One; Tobias Follings of Ridge Number Two; Frank Simms of Ridge Number Three. Lieutenant Bridges commanded the mounted reserves, and George Macklin was in charge of the covered wagon contingent.

In the distance to the east, it was possible to see the vanguard of the Brown Shirt army, moving slowly up the road toward their position. The single plane left to Corvallo was circling high overhead, engaging in observation only. No doubt, when the two armies clashed, that ship would do its bits in strafing the defenders of the ridge. But now it was merely taking stock of their positions.

Jimmy Christopher talked in a low voice to Delcourt and his lieutenants. "These three ridges command the valley," he was saying, "so that we can't be attacked on the flank. But the enemy has artillery, and that's what I'm afraid of. Also, they have odds of six to one in their favor." He paused. "I might as well tell you, gentlemen, that I have no real hope of victory. The only thing I can promise you is the chance to die like Americans."

REVOLT OF THE DEVIL MEN

Delcourt nodded gravely. "Every one of the boys who volunteered knows that as well as we do. Just give them that chance, Operator 5. Perhaps, if we put up a good fight here, it'll inspire others to do the same elsewhere, instead of knuckling under to the Brown Shirts. And if a wave of resistance builds up in America, no dictator can stand against us. Let us just do that—and we will not have died in vain!"

"Amen!" said Jimmy Christopher. He removed his hat, and knelt on the ground. The other did likewise. The riflemen in the trenches, as well as the mounted cavalry behind the ridges, seeing what Operator 5 was doing, joined him.

Jimmy Christopher raised his bared head to clear sky overhead, and spoke a short prayer to the Almighty.

A great silence fell upon those hard-bitten plainsmen and hunters as Jimmy spoke the words they could not hear. But they knew that he was not speaking to a Lord of Hosts, demanding victory. They felt that he was talking to a benign and understanding Providence, asking only that peace might come at last to a world in turmoil.

When he finished, he bowed his head for a moment, and then arose. And it seemed that his words, spoken sincerely, and in all humility, were heard.

For almost upon the heels of that prayer a great droning sound filled the sky. A tremor went through the entrenched riflemen, Operator 5, Hugh Delcourt and the others. It seemed to them that a great voice was answering them out of the vast firmament.

Their questing eyes, darting upward, settled upon a huge

OPERATOR 5

The American riflemen came charging out of their positions!

REVOLT OF THE DEVIL MEN

OPERATOR 5

winged machine that came sloping down out of the clouds, trim, sleek and graceful. In a way that great bomber, which their wondering gaze rested upon, was really a portent of Heaven.

After the first moment of wonder, an audible sigh rose from those in the trenches. For the bold colors of the union flag of Great Britain were clearly discernible on the under part of the mighty spreading wings of the giant ship.

Operator 5 gripped the arm of Hugh Delcourt. "It's a Handley-Page bomber!" he exclaimed. It's a land plane, but it flies the Navy insignia. Delcourt, that means that the British have sent the fleet they promised us!"

Delcourt's eyes were filled with a religious awe, and he trembled. "It was meant to happen this way!" he whispered. "God was testing us. We were ready to die for a principle; and now we have a chance to prevail!"

THEY WATCHED while the great Handey-Page circled low overhead, inspecting the Hawk flag of the Brown Shirt army, and the Stars and Stripes which floated over Ridges One, Two and Three. Then the bomber circled once more, headed into the wind, and nosed down toward the field between Ridge One and Ridge Two.

A few moments later she was sliding gracefully along the ground to a perfect landing. Three uniformed men descended. One wore the full-dress uniform of a rear admiral of the imperial navy of Great Britain; another—the pilot—wore the uniform of a major of the Royal Air Force, while the third was a sergeant-mechanic.

Operator 5 met them near the ship. In a moment, he was

shaking hands, introducing himself, and being informed of the identity of the visitors. "Rear Admiral Sir Jelliffe-Osborne, sir. And this is Major Crowe, of the Royal Air Force. Operator 5, we have made good our promise to you. I have a fleet of nine vessels in the harbor at Galveston." Sir Jelliffe-Osborne cast a glance across at the enemy lines. "The rumors we heard in England were well informed, then?"

Operator 5 nodded. "Had you come three days earlier, Sir Jelliffe-Osborne, we could have used your services. As it is, I'm afraid you're in time to see the end of democracy in America. There's the opening gun of the battle!"

The Brown Shirt batteries were plainly in sight, and they could see the puffs of smoke that burst as the enemy went into action. The air was suddenly filled with screaming shells. They were too high, and burst far beyond the American lines, but it was plain to see that General Corvallo was trying to hit the British plane. He wanted to put it out of commission lest it join in the battle on the side of Operator 5.

Sir Jelliffe-Osborne groaned. "If they'd only delayed opening the battle! I could have brought up a couple of big guns—"

Jimmy Christopher shrugged. "It's the fortune of war, sir. I thank you on behalf of the American people for your kindness. And I suggest that you return to the fleet. There's no sense in you being killed."

Sir Jelliffe-Osborne glared at Jimmy Christopher. "I'll be damned if I'll do anything of the sort, sir! England owes you a greater debt than she can pay. Had it not been for the persistence and courage of you Yankees, the Purple Empire would still be the mistress of our lives, and England would not now be a free country. We're going to repay that debt by helping you beat this dictator!"

"But how?" Jimmy demanded. He had no hope of substantial aid from the British navy, six hundred miles away in Galveston. Before they could bring their big guns up, the battle would be over.

But Sir Jelliffe-Osborne was smiling across at Major Crowe, as if enjoying a secret joke.

Jimmy was impatient to leave them and take over command of the defenses. The enemy's shells were coming over fast now, and the air was thick with thunder of the cannonading. Though they had not yet succeeded in getting the range, they would certainly shorten fire, and blast his riflemen out of their shallow trenches. Jimmy wanted to order them to move back behind the ridge, for greater protection, but he paused a moment, looking from the Admiral to Major Crowe, suddenly sensing that they had something important to tell him.

It was Major Crowe who smilingly gave him the news. "We have not come alone, Operator 5. Among our fleet, there is an airplane carrier. Right now, a flotilla of six bombers like this, each carrying a full load of bombs, is following us here. They should arrive within twenty minutes!"

Jimmy Christopher's eyes widened. A surge of joy ran through him. It was the thing he had least expected. Six bombers like this one would turn the tide from defeat to victory.

Hugh Delcourt, who had been standing beside him, suddenly let out a whoop. "Hooray for the British Navy!"

Operator 5 swung into action. He motioned to an orderly. "My compliments to Captain Bretton. Instruct him to withdraw the riflemen from the trenches to new positions behind the Ridges. Tell him the Royal Air Force is on the way!"

A shell hit less than a hundred feet from them, and the explosion smashed against their eardrums. A great spume of earth shot up like a geyser, leaving a wide gash in the ground. Another shell, and another, fell nearer....

"They're finding the range!" Jimmy said hurriedly. "I think you'd better get up in the air, Major Crowe."

"Righto!" said the major. "I'll drop a few eggs on their batteries. Hold your lines for twenty minutes, Operator 5, till my planes get here!"

Jimmy watched him take off, with Admiral Sir Jelliffe-Osborne in the observer's cockpit, prepared to operate the bomb-release levers, and grinning as if he was enjoying the whole thing immensely.

JIMMY MOUNTED his horse, and, in company with Delcourt, moved away toward the top of the ridge. Now that the British plane had taken off, the Brown Shirt batteries changed their objective to the top of Ridge One, and Jimmy was glad that he had ordered the withdrawal of his riflemen. They would never have survived that deadly barrage.

Suddenly, Delcourt reached over and gripped Jimmy's arm. He pointed excitedly out toward the field between the two armies and raised his voice in a hoarse shout to make himself heard above the thunder of the guns.

"Look, Operator 5! Who in God's name is that?"

OPERATOR 5

The distance between the vanguard of the Brown Shirt army and the foot of Ridge One was perhaps a quarter of a mile, across a wide field which Operator 5 had caused to be studded with barbed wire. At the far end of this field, the infantry of the Brown Shirts could be seen through the swirling clouds of smoke, ready to charge as soon as the barrage lifted. The outlines of the three tanks were also visible, rolling slowly forward.

But it was not at these that Delcourt was pointing. His trembling finger indicated the single horse that now came racing across that field, virtually from out of the enemy ranks, and heading directly toward them. There seemed to be two riders on the horse. One was seated, erect, the other apparently tied to the saddle, lying athwart the pommel. That they were escaping from the enemy lines was plain, for already a hail of lead followed them from the rifles of the Brown Shirt snipers. One of the tanks seemed to be gathering momentum to follow that horse.

Swiftly, pale with a sudden premonition, Operator 5 lifted his glasses, focusing them upon the horse and its two riders. A sudden surge of happiness went through him. That was Diane Elliot sitting in the saddle, bending low, spurring the horse on furiously! Across the pommel lay the unconscious, slight figure of Tim Donovan, head hanging over the side, a bloody bandage on his shoulder!

Tim and Diane alive! That first thought that flashed through Jimmy Christopher's mind. Something awoke within him—a spark which he had believed forever dead….

NEXT INSTANT he was acutely aware of the danger snapping at the heels of those two whom he loved. Delcourt, who had raised his own glasses, groaned aloud. "They'll never make it! That horse is spent already! It'll never carry them!"

Jimmy Christopher didn't hear him, because he was already a dozen feet away, spurring out into the field.

He urged his horse forward, leaping the barbed-wire entanglements which he had placed here, himself, to hamper the enemy but which now threatened to ruin all chance of escape for Diane and Tim. He could see Diane fighting to get the last ounce of effort out of her mount. The weary steed balked, time and again, at jumping the barbed-wire. She had to swerve and go around, while bullets from the enemy rifles whipped about her, and the tank lumbered after them in a straight line, flattening down the barbed-wire, effortlessly.

Jimmy Christopher's blood was racing, and there was a great ache in his heart. Had he regained hope for those two, only to see them die before his eyes? The horse would never carry both Diane and the unconscious Tim across that field!

His only chance was to get to them before their horse fell, and the tank reached them. He bent low over his horse's mane, urging it ahead with every muscle of his body.

A shell exploded between himself and the two. He groaned. The enemy had turned one of its big guns on the field. The shell dug up a huge crater where it exploded. Diane swerved so as not to head for it. Now there was perhaps two hundred yards between Jimmy and Diane. The tank was about the same distance behind her, its machine gun poking forward, waiting for the opportunity to cut her down. Her horse was faltering. The weight of both was too much for it.

OPERATOR 5

And then it was that Operator 5, and all the watching Americans of both armies, saw performed before their eyes one of the most heroic and self-sacrificing deeds that it is the privilege of man to witness. They saw Diane deliberately draw in the reins to slow up the horse, swing a leg over the side, jump to the ground—and slap the animal's flank. The steed, relieved of the excess weight, leaped ahead and raced freely toward the American lines, away from the pounding artillery of the Brown Shirts. Tim Donovan's hundred-odd pounds were easily carried by it, and it bore the unconscious lad safely toward Ridge One, where eager hands seized him. Diane's act of self-sacrifice had saved the boy!

But Diane Elliot had virtually given up her life to do it. When she had leaped from the horse, she was directly alongside the shellhole just gouged into the ground. Swirling smoke had prevented her from seeing it, and, instead of landing on level ground, she fell into the crater.

Jimmy's lips were drawn into a tight line as he raced toward her. He saw her push up from the hole, try to climb out, fall back. He saw her try again but knew why she couldn't make it. She was entangled with the barbed wire which the shell had smashed into the hole. *She couldn't get out!*

Behind her now, less than a hundred feet away, the tank rumbled on, its driver gleefully aiming the tread so that it would drop into the hole, crush her alive.

Even while he raced toward Diane, Jimmy Christopher glimpsed that face behind the shatter-proof glass of the tank, and the veins stood out on his forehead. That was Blaintree, himself, driving the tank that was to crush life from Diane's body!

Frantically, Jimmy spurred his horse forward. He reached that shellhole and flung himself down, drawing the saber from the scabbard at his horse's side. Diane saw him come, looked up, and a great tenderness came in her eyes.

"Jimmy! You can't get me out in time. That tank! It's almost on us. Leave me—

He grinned tightly and slashed at the barbed wire—great, desperate hackings, that bit and ripped. Then he leaped into the hole, fought with the barbs tearing at Diane's white body.

"Jimmy! Leave me—"

"Never, darling!"

And now the tank loomed above them, thirty… twenty-five feet away. He saw that it was useless. He couldn't free her in time. His eyes burned; his hands were raw and bleeding from the barbs. He drew his gun. "One for you… one for me, Diane. It's better than being crushed—"

His words were drowned in a thunderous detonation that drove the blood pounding in their veins and almost burst their eardrums. A shadow, swooping low, passed over them, droning, roaring, then zooming upward. And where the tank had been there was a great geyser of smoke and, in a moment, only bits of steel, bodies, human flesh that came raining down upon them!

IT WAS several minutes before Diane regained her senses. She awoke on the ground, with Jimmy Christopher leaning over her, smiling. "Jimmy! What happened?"

He kissed her. "Good old Major Crowe! I'd forgotten him,

darling. He dived on that tank and dropped one of his eggs on it. Blew the thing into the sky. That was the end of Blaintree, too!"

It was also the end of the battle of Santa Fe. For at the moment when the Handley-Page had zoomed over Blaintree's tank, six other Handley's had come above over the battlefield. Crowe zoomed upward, took his position at the head of the formation, and swung his arm in a wide, eloquent signal. Then those bombers went to work in earnest. For ten minutes, they flew back and forth over the Brown Shirt array, dropping their loads of deadly explosive. Before they were through, the battalions of General Corvallo were in full flight.

With a *whoop* the American riflemen came charging out of their positions. But they had not covered fifty feet before the cavalry came out from behind the ridge, and outstripped them. The cavalry reached the enemy first, smashing home the victory, routing them completely.

Jimmy Christopher kissed Diane again, and left her there on the field. He had mounted in time to lead that cavalry charge—and it was his whistle that sounded the recall. The enemy was beaten. There was no use in needless slaughter, for those men were also Americans and many of them only misguided, others conscripted.

With the guiding evil genius of the Brown Shirts gone, there was no longer danger to the liberty of America....

But the next morning, with the rising of the sun, two men were marched out to the field to face a firing-squad. They were Corvallo and Godkin.

Grimly, Jimmy Christopher refused them mercy. And as he

heard the shots of the firing squad, he murmured, "Hank, they weren't good enough to wipe your boots!"

Then, misty-eyed, he turned back to the multitudinous duties that lay before him, and the one duty that he was grimly determined to fulfill to the letter—making utterly safe for democracy the country which Hank Sheridan had given his life to preserve as a free and happy nation!*

---

* AUTHOR'S NOTE: The overthrowing of the Brown Shirts, by Operator 5 and his gallant patriots, was a heroic—but, sad to say—inconclusive act in the history of our country during those troublous times. It was in the very midst of his triumph, following the defeat of Blaintree's dastardly scheme, that Operator 5 received the curiously garbled communication from the West that told him America, once more, was being subjected to foreign menace. It was this discovery which led to his decision to journey to Europe with a Suicide Battalion, in a hair-raising attempt to forestall the most dastardly unprovoked attack in history—by a combine of outlaw nations who had gone mad with the thirst for conquest… the dramatic account of this daring undercover invasion—and of the brief but bloody war which followed—to be told in the next installment.

POPULAR HERO PULPS AVAILABLE NOW:

THE SPIDER
- ❏ #1: The Spider Strikes — $13.95
- ❏ #2: The Wheel of Death — $13.95
- ❏ #3: Wings of the Black Death — $13.95
- ❏ #4: City of Flaming Shadows — $13.95
- ❏ #5: Empire of Doom! — $13.95
- ❏ #6: Citadel of Hell — $13.95
- ❏ #7: The Serpent of Destruction — $13.95
- ❏ #8: The Mad Horde — $13.95
- ❏ #9: Satan's Death Blast — $13.95
- ❏ #10: The Corpse Cargo — $13.95
- ❏ #11: Prince of the Red Looters — $13.95
- ❏ #12: Reign of the Silver Terror — $13.95
- ❏ #13: Builders of the Dark Empire — $13.95
- ❏ #14: Death's Crimson Juggernaut — $13.95
- ❏ #15: The Red Death Rain — $13.95
- ❏ #16: The City Destroyer — $13.95
- ❏ #17: The Pain Emperor — $13.95
- ❏ #18: The Flame Master — $13.95
- ❏ #19: Slaves of the Crime Master — $13.95
- ❏ #20: Reign of the Death Fiddler — $13.95
- ❏ #21: Hordes of the Red Butcher — $13.95
- ❏ #22: Dragon Lord of the Underworld — $13.95
- ❏ #23: Master of the Death-Madness — $13.95
- ❏ #24: King of the Red Killers — $13.95
- ❏ #25: Overlord of the Damned — $13.95
- ❏ #26: Death Reign of the Vampire King — $13.95
- ❏ #27: Emperor of the Yellow Death — $13.95
- ❏ #28: The Mayor of Hell — $13.95
- ❏ #29: Slaves of the Murder Syndicate — $13.95
- ❏ #30: Green Globes of Death — $13.95
- ❏ #31: The Cholera King — $13.95
- ❏ #32: Slaves of the Dragon — $13.95
- ❏ #33: Legions of Madness — $12.95
- ❏ #34: Laboratory of the Damned — $12.95
- ❏ #35: Satan's Sightless Legion — $12.95
- ❏ #36: The Coming of the Terror — $12.95
- ❏ #37: The Devil's Death-Dwarfs — $12.95
- ❏ #38: City of Dreadful Night — $12.95
- ❏ #39: Reign of the Snake Men — $12.95
- ❏ #40: Dictator of the Damned — $12.95
- ❏ #41: The Mill-Town Massacres — $12.95
- ❏ #42: Satan's Workshop — $12.95
- ❏ #43: Scourge of the Yellow Fangs — $12.95
- ❏ #44: The Devil's Pawnbroker — $12.95
- ❏ #45: Voyage of the Coffin Ship — $12.95
- ❏ #46: The Man Who Ruled in Hell — $13.95
- ❏ #47: Slaves of the Black Monarch — $13.95
- ❏ #48: Machineguns Over the White House — $13.95
- ❏ #49: The City That Dared Not Eat — $13.95
- ❏ #50: Master of the Flaming Horde — $13.95
- ❏ #51: Satan's Switchboard — $13.95
- ❏ #52: Legions of the Accursed Light — $13.95
- ❏ #53: The City of Lost Men — $13.95
- ❏ #54: The Grey Horde Creeps — $13.95
- ❏ #55: City of Whispering Death — $13.95
- ❏ #56: When Thousands Slept in Hell — $13.95
- ❏ #57: Satan's Shakles — $14.95
- ❏ #58: The Emperor From Hell — $14.95
- ❏ #59: The Devil's Candlesticks — $14.95
- ❏ #60: The City That Paid to Die — $14.95
- ❏ #61: The Spider at Bay — $14.95
- ❏ #62: Scourge of the Black Legions — $14.95
- ❏ #63: The Withering Death — $14.95
- ❏ #64: Claws of the Golden Dragon — $14.95
- ❏ #65: The Song of Death — $14.95
- ❏ #66: The Silver Death Reign — $14.95
- ❏ #67: Blight of the Blazing Eye — $14.95
- ❏ #68: King of the Fleshless Legion — $14.95
- ❏ #69: Rule of the Monster Men — $16.95
- ❏ #70: The Spider and the Slaves of Hell — $16.95
- ❏ **NEW:** #71: The Spider and the Fire God — $16.95

THE WESTERN RAIDER
- ❏ #1: Guns of the Damned — $13.95
- ❏ #2: The Hawk Rides Back from Death — $13.95
- ❏ #3: Gun-Call for the Lost Legion — $13.95
- ❏ #4: The Law of Silver Trent — $13.95
- ❏ #5: The Gun-Prayer of Silver Trent — $13.95
- ❏ #6: Silver Trent Rides Alone — $13.95

G-8 AND HIS BATTLE ACES
- ❏ #1: The Bat Staffel — $13.95

CAPTAIN SATAN
- ❏ #1: The Mask of the Damned — $13.95
- ❏ #2: Parole for the Dead — $13.95
- ❏ #3: The Dead Man Express — $13.95
- ❏ #4: A Ghost Rides the Dawn — $13.95
- ❏ #5: The Ambassador From Hell — $13.95

DR. YEN SIN
- ❏ #1: Mystery of the Dragon's Shadow — $12.95
- ❏ #2: Mystery of the Golden Skull — $12.95
- ❏ #3: Mystery of the Singing Mummies — $12.95

RED FINGER
- ❏ **NEW:** #1: Second-Hand Death — $24.95

POPULAR HERO PULPS AVAILABLE NOW:

ACE G-MAN
- ❑ #1: The Suicide Squad Reports for Death — $14.95
- ❑ #2: Coffins for the Suicide Squad — $14.95
- ❑ #3: Shells for the Suicide Squad — $14.95
- ❑ #4: The Suicide Squad in Corpse-Town — $14.95
- ❑ #5: Wanted–In Three Pine Coffins — $14.95
- ❑ #6: The Suicide Squad's Dawn Patrol — $14.95
- ❑ **NEW:** #7: Targets for the Flaming Arrow — $16.95

OPERATOR 5
- ❑ #1: The Masked Invasion — $13.95
- ❑ #2: The Invisible Empire — $13.95
- ❑ #3: The Yellow Scourge — $13.95
- ❑ #4: The Melting Death — $13.95
- ❑ #5: Cavern of the Damned — $13.95
- ❑ #6: Master of Broken Men — $13.95
- ❑ #7: Invasion of the Dark Legions — $13.95
- ❑ #8: The Green Death Mists — $13.95
- ❑ #9: Legions of Starvation — $13.95
- ❑ #10: The Red Invader — $13.95
- ❑ #11: The League of War-Monsters — $13.95
- ❑ #12: The Army of the Dead — $13.95
- ❑ #13: March of the Flame Marauders — $13.95
- ❑ #14: Blood Reign of the Dictator — $13.95
- ❑ #15: Invasion of the Yellow Warlords — $13.95
- ❑ #16: Legions of the Death Master — $13.95
- ❑ #17: Hosts of the Flaming Death — $13.95
- ❑ #18: Invasion of the Crimson Death Cult — $13.95
- ❑ #19: Attack of the Blizzard Men — $13.95
- ❑ #20: Scourge of the Invisible Death — $13.95
- ❑ #21: Raiders of the Red Death — $13.95
- ❑ #22: War-Dogs of the Green Destroyer — $13.95
- ❑ #23: Rockets From Hell — $13.95
- ❑ #24: War-Masters from the Orient — $13.95
- ❑ #25: Crime's Reign of Terror — $13.95
- ❑ #26: Death's Ragged Army — $13.95
- ❑ #27: Patriots' Death Battalion — $13.95
- ❑ #28: The Bloody Forty-five Days — $13.95
- ❑ #29: America's Plague Battalions — $13.95
- ❑ #30: Liberty's Suicide Legions — $13.95
- ❑ #31: Siege of the Thousand Patriots — $13.95
- ❑ #32: Patriots' Death March — $14.95
- ❑ #33: Revolt of the Lost Legions — $14.95
- ❑ #34: Drums of Destruction — $14.95
- ❑ #35: The Army Without a Country — $14.95
- ❑ #36: The Bloody Frontiers — $14.95
- ❑ #37: The Coming of the Mongol Hordes — $14.95
- ❑ #38: The Siege That Brought the Black Death — $16.95
- ❑ **NEW:** #39: Revolt of the Devil Men — $16.95

CAPTAIN COMBAT
- ❑ #1: The Sky Beast of Berlin — $13.95
- ❑ #2: Red Wings For the Blood Battalion — $13.95
- ❑ #3: Low Ceiling For Nazi Hell Hawks — $13.95

DUSTY AYRES AND HIS BATTLE BIRDS
- ❑ #1: Black Lightning! — $13.95
- ❑ #2: Crimson Doom — $13.95
- ❑ #3: The Purple Tornado — $13.95
- ❑ #4: The Screaming Eye — $13.95
- ❑ #5: The Green Thunderbolt — $13.95
- ❑ #6: The Red Destroyer — $13.95
- ❑ #7: The White Death — $13.95
- ❑ #8: The Black Avenger — $13.95
- ❑ #9: The Silver Typhoon — $13.95
- ❑ #10: The Troposphere F-S — $13.95
- ❑ #11: The Blue Cyclone — $13.95
- ❑ #12: The Tesla Raiders — $13.95

MAVERICKS
- ❑ #1: Five Against the Law — $12.95
- ❑ #2: Mesquite Manhunters — $12.95
- ❑ #3: Bait for the Lobo Pack — $12.95
- ❑ #4: Doc Grimson's Outlaw Posse — $12.95
- ❑ #5: Charlie Parr's Gunsmoke Cure — $12.95

THE MYSTERIOUS WU FANG
- ❑ #1: The Case of the Six Coffins — $12.95
- ❑ #2: The Case of the Scarlet Feather — $12.95
- ❑ #3: The Case of the Yellow Mask — $12.95
- ❑ #4: The Case of the Suicide Tomb — $12.95
- ❑ #5: The Case of the Green Death — $12.95
- ❑ #6: The Case of the Black Lotus — $12.95
- ❑ #7: The Case of the Hidden Scourge — $12.95

THE SECRET 6
- ❑ #1: The Red Shadow — $13.95
- ❑ #2: House of Walking Corpses — $13.95
- ❑ #3: The Monster Murders — $13.95
- ❑ #4: The Golden Alligator — $13.95

CAPTAIN ZERO
- ❑ #1: City of Deadly Sleep — $13.95
- ❑ #2: The Mark of Zero! — $13.95
- ❑ #3: The Golden Murder Syndicate — $13.95